ARTHUR BANNER

This novel is entirely a work of fiction although some of the historical details and characters are factual. Persons and companies named within the script are fictional and are the product of the author's imagination. Apart from those in the public domain, any similarity to persons past or living is coincidental.

CONTENTS

I wish to thank my wife for her support and understanding, while I was researching and writing this story and subsequently for proofreading it, so that I could correct some of my errors and omissions.

1. PREFACE

This story has been woven around true events and was real for the characters involved, although they only lived in the author's mind.

The maps, which have been included, are not to scale and include roads which did not exist at the time of the Spanish Civil War. The intention is merely to help those, who are unfamiliar with Spain, to follow the journey. Readers are recommended to refer to Michelin maps for accurate modern information.

2. ANDALUCÍA

Introducing the Garcías…

Leo García Díaz was a sturdy twenty-five-year-old of above average height. His handsome face had laughter lines pointing to his dark eyes, which the ladies especially, found deeply engaging. He usually wore a white open-necked shirt and black waistcoat with black trousers. He spoke clearly but with an Andalusian accent. With his relaxed confident manner he had a way of entertaining those around him. Leo owned a bar in Baena which is south east of Córdoba city.

Carla García Díaz, (Leo's sister), was quite tall, with an attractive figure and slender legs. She had a slim neck rising to a pale-complexioned face, framed by beautiful long black hair. Her almond-shaped hazel eyes sparkled like her personality, but concealed her vulnerability to poor health.

Their Mother and Father: Teresa and Vicente.
Leo's Bar Assistant: Ana.

And the Sánchez…

José Sánchez Moreno was a vigorous 23-year-old, with

bronzed skin, dark brown eyes and straight black hair, with a few strands falling over his right eye. Despite his slim appearance, he had broad shoulders, muscular arms and large hands. His family owned a local vineyard. José's education included understudying the vineyard's foreman, but at harvest time his father taught him about blending and producing the wine.

Rosa Sánchez Diaz was the daughter from the marriage of José and Carla.

José's Mother and Father: Alicia and Eduardo.

Happy Moments in Terrible Times for the Garcias and Sánchez. Their story begins near Baena, in the province of Córdoba.

José and Carla were married and moved into an almost derelict farmhouse which José had inherited. With help from the family, they soon made it their home. On 11th May 1931, Carla gave birth to a little girl.

José presented Carla with a single red rose, bent down and kissed her and their daughter. With tears in her eyes, Carla said, *"Let's call her Rosa!"*

Later, at Rosa's christening, fewer people attended than normal because of the social unrest and José's reluctance to show any false sign of apparent wealth. Their grandparents agreed and thought he was right to be careful.

From her first smile, her first little chuckle, her first step, Rosa seemed to know how to charm people. Initially, she used words sparingly, because, of course, she didn't know many. However, she quickly learned which words and phrases were rewarded with a loving smile and she never seemed to be without a willing audience.

As a child, she wasn't aware of her mother's slow deterioration in health. Neither did she know of the increasing turmoil outside her own little world.

Ana, (Leo's bar assistant), had a nephew, called Miguel, a gangly youth who was looking for work. Vicente and Theresa took on the fifteen-year-old boy, in Carla's absence. He was a willing to learn new skills, and although he quickly became Vicente's shadow, he could be relied upon to work independently when needed. This gave Teresa the opportunity to visit Carla and Rosa, and sometimes see Leo in his bar.

Poverty and discontent were widespread in the province of Córdoba and the depressed Spanish economy worsened with the Wall Street Crash. Then, in January 1930, Spain's military dictator resigned, King Alfonso XIII abdicated and the Second Spanish Republic was created, with the country being governed by disagreeing Republican, Socialist, Anarchist and Communist factions. From 1933 to 1935, the volatile government became more right wing and a civil war seemed more and more likely due to increasing violence and reprisals among the differing factions.

Those troubles hadn't yet come to their doorstep, but they were coming closer... how safe were they?

Towards the end of 1934, Ana's husband died from a lung infection. At first, she tried to keep the bakery going but it was too much for her. Nobody could afford to buy it, so she and Leo locked up, removed the contents, and took them to the García farm for Leo's mother.

Ana was a well-proportioned jolly lady, about seven years his senior. Wearing her wrap-round apron over a print dress, she also attended the customers with a motherly competent manner and excelled in looking after all the bar food.

Fortunately, Leo had a spare room above the bar and he asked Ana to move in and work for him as long as she wanted. They were both content with the new arrangement and, as time went by, Leo was able to make more frequent visits to his parents, his sister and Rosa.

On 11th May 1936, there was a small party for Rosa's fifth birthday. She had a good time and the adults enjoyed hearing her laughing and singing. However, after the party, the adults exchanged worrying pieces of news and it was agreed that everyone felt a nervous sense of waiting. WAITING for the storm cloud to break!

The conflict begins

The increasing aggression throughout Spain exploded a month after Rosa's birthday, with shootings and reprisals in Madrid.

Early in July, the press announced new controversial regulations for rural work. As a result, about 200 landowners went en mass to Córdoba city to protest to the Governor.

Compounding this, the unions commenced strike action.

Encouraged by the Guardia Civil, most of the landowners were now armed with rifles and prominent Nationalists were appointed as guards to patrol Baena.

Nationalist Rebels took Morocco and the Canary Islands.

On 17th July 1936, Franco declared a State of War …

Within less than a week, Franco's Nationalists held Cádiz, Sevilla, several major cities in the north and there was street fighting in Barcelona and Madrid… In Toledo, the Nationalists had taken hostages and were under siege in the castle.

THE STORM CLOUD HAD BURST WITH A VENGEANCE!

The Atrocities in Baena

Before the end of July 1936, chaos hit Baena. It was about 4 o'clock in the afternoon and Leo was about to open up after the siesta break.

Hundreds of workers marched on the town. They were armed mostly with farm tools, but some had rifles. They attacked the nearby Guardia Civil barracks but were repelled. The Guardia Civil consolidated their defence, but the attackers had the barracks surrounded. Throughout the ensuing skirmishes, Leo kept the shutters closed and the doors locked.

Leo and Ana went upstairs and looked out through half-closed shutters. They couldn't see much and didn't want to spend too much time by the windows, but the noise of people and guns intensified and then reduced to sporadic gunfire and shouting.

Leo asked Ana to collect her essential things in a bag, while he did the same.

"Stay up here Ana ... I'm just going to check downstairs!"

From under the bar counter, he collected his hunting knife and sheath, then emptied the cash drawer into a bag.

On returning upstairs, he took out his reserve money from a cache in his bedroom, put all the money into a haversack with the rest of his essentials and looked around the room.

"*Ana ... Are you dressed and ready to make an emergency exit?*"

"*Yes, Leo, you say the word; I'm ready when you are!*"

They took two-hour shifts through the night, with one downstairs staying awake and the other upstairs sleeping fitfully or pretending to sleep.

A few hours after daybreak, they were both in the kitchen at the back of the premises when there was urgent knocking on the back door. Nervously, Leo opened the little door set at eye level in the bigger door … standing there was one of his regular customers.

"*Let me in, it's not safe out here!*"

Leo let him in and immediately re-closed and bolted the door, before asking, "*What's going on out there?*"

With a large measure of alcohol in his shaking hand, the visitor explained that some miners had come up with the idea of making a large hole in the walls between the terraced houses near the town square. This would enable them to come and go closer to the edge of the siege without being seen or shot. He nervously added that he had been sent ahead to warn any occupants that they shouldn't try to stop the miners.

Leo thanked him, gave him a bottle of anís, and while letting him out, saw two Molotov cocktails hit his van which was parked in the access lane. That ruled out his plan to escape in the van!

Should they wait for their escape route to appear

before them, in the form of a hole in the wall?

"If it works for them, let it work for us," said Leo philosophically.

So they waited and waited until there was a loud hammering on the wall. A small hole appeared, then it became bigger and a rifle came through, followed by a man. *"Stand back, we're coming through!"*

Four armed men came through the hole and a few words were gruffly exchanged, Leo said, *"We'll leave you to your tunnelling!"*

He crawled through the hole, with Ana right behind him, each firmly grasping their bag of essentials.

The couple went from one empty house or shop to another until they reached the end of the terrace. From there, they were in the open, but not out of the danger zone. To avoid a couple of angry mobs, Leo pulled Ana into some shrubbery until they moved on. They were less hesitant when they reached the outskirts of town, but by this time it was getting dark.

For safety, they took refuge in an old derelict building and in the morning, they walked the rest of the way to José and Carla's home."

When they staggered through José and Carla's front door, Leo and Ana were exhausted, dishevelled and dirty … José sat them at the table and Carla made some breakfast.

Leo began in a low mumble, *"Have you heard that the Guardia are under siege in Baena town centre? Somebody burned my van … The Leftists made big holes in the walls of adjoining houses right through to the bar, so that they could move closer to the town centre without being shot in the streets ... We escaped through the holes they had knocked out!"*

"How did you get here?" asked José.

"We walked until it was dark and sheltered in an old barn for the night ... Today; we walked the rest of the way here!"

Carla put some food on the table. *"You must be hungry ... Here! ... I'm making coffee."*

"My God!" said Leo. As he finished his coffee, he looked at José, *"Do you have your motorbike here?"*

"Well... Yes!"

"Can I borrow it? I must warn Papa not to do his rounds. He normally goes today."

But, the moment he said it, Vicente's van could be heard. He entered and was surprised to see Leo and Ana. *"What's happened?"*

José sat Vicente at the table. Carla poured more coffee and Vicente looked at the worried faces around him. Leo then retold his story.

"Ana and I can't go back to town. Please take us home with you..."

"Of course, my boy, we must warn your mother and make sure Ana's nephew doesn't go into town."

They left right away and on arrival at the García farm, Teresa rushed out. *"What's wrong? Tell me what's happened!"*

Leo told their story once more and Teresa immediately exclaimed breathlessly, *"Miguel has a couple of days off and, an hour ago, he left on his bicycle to go and see his parents at their shop by the town square ... It's too late to stop him!"*

"Oh poor boy, I hope he's safe."

In her usual cotton dress, apron and slippers, Teresa sat for a while, in shocked silence, nervously flicking back wisps of hair from her rounded face. She looked firstly at Vicente, then at Leo and Ana.

She suddenly stood up and, talking incessantly, busied herself organising sleeping arrangements for Ana.

"You're so kind," said Ana, *"Let me help with those things, Leo! Come and help us move these heavy things!"*

*

As Miguel approached the outskirts of town, he could hear shouting and sporadic gunfire. When he was in the suburbs, he dismounted and pushed his bike from one street corner to the next, checking carefully, before moving on. He eventually made it to his parents' shop where they had closed the shutters. He went round the back and banged on the door until his father let him in. He took his bike in with him and it was clear that they were petrified. They had locked themselves in the shop, waiting for the bedlam outside to end.

Miguel's father explained that the barracks seemed to be under siege from Leftists who had set up their headquarters in the nearby convent.

The family spent several more nights hiding quietly in the store room, while they listened fearfully to the sounds of skirmishing in the street and occasional explosions from the direction of the Guardia Civil barracks.

Miguel's father reckoned it must have been after about eight nights that they had spent there, when they heard heavy vehicles, an increase in gunfire and enormous screaming and shouting followed by more gunfire.

The Nationalists inside the barracks had received massive reinforcements. A column including Legionnaires, Infantry, Artillery and Guardia Civil had left from Córdoba at dawn. The siege was over.

When, timidly, the family opened the door and looked outside in the street, they stood on the threshold in stunned silence.

The Guardia Civil Lieutenant had led his men from the barracks and was directing a hellish retribution on the townsfolk. People were being forced to lay face-down, side by side, in the Town Hall square. He led the killing of so many people, that the corpses seemed to fill the square and their blood ran in the gutters. Horse-drawn carts then came and the bodies were taken to the cemetery and burned in heaps. This was repeated again and again.

Meanwhile, the relief soldiers, many of them extremists from the Moroccan campaign, looted the houses and brought more victims for the bloody slaughter.

Miguel retreated back inside and said insistently, *"Hurry! Come back into the shop!"*

But before they could move, one of the Guardia appeared and grabbed his father saying, *"You've been supplying the Union bastards!"*

*

Miguel's mother collapsed against the door, shutting Miguel inside. Miguel's ten-year-old sister pleaded with the Guard and held his jacket. The Guard hit her across the face and knocked her to the ground. Another couple of Guards joined in and brutally manhandled the three into the square. They were told to lay face-down with the others.

Miguel locked the door again and peered through a gap in the shutters. He saw the Lieutenant shoot his mother, father and little sister … each one in the back of the neck while they lay face down. Miguel went into a catatonic trance for some time before stumbling back into the storeroom where he slumped to the floor and sobbed himself to sleep in the dark room.

When he wakened, it was dark outside.

He wondered if his Aunt Ana was OK, so he gingerly went from doorway to doorway until he reached Leo's bar where he heard raucous laughter. Bravely, or stupidly, he opened the door and looked inside.

A Legionnaire saw him, *"What do you want, boy?"*

"I was looking for my aunt!" Miguel looked round the room to see a burly Moor boasting to his friends while holding up some of Ana's jewellery and some other trinkets,

"I got these upstairs, there was nobody there, so now these are mine!"

Miguel looked back at the Legionnaire and mumbled, *"Thanks."*

"She's not here!"

He made a rapid exit and raced down the street in terror, throwing caution to the wind. Back at the shop, he calmed down, collected his bike and pedalled nervously from one block to the next until he was out of town.

Some miners, standing by a truck, stopped him.

They saw he was no threat and how scared he was. They gave him some water and chatted to calm him. Miguel was told that about eighty hostages had been murdered by workers before they left their headquarters in the convent. The miners were waiting to see if any more of their group had escaped from the town.

Miguel was asked if he wanted to travel with them to their village. He declined, and said he was nearly home. They wished him luck and he didn't stop again until he reached the García farm and knocked on their door.

Leo flung the door open. He stood, with a shotgun in his hands, looking at Miguel and into the darkness beyond. Ana and Mr and Mrs García were in the living room behind him.

The homely glow enveloped Miguel and he fainted on the doorstep.

They carried the lad inside and gently revived him. He looked at Ana and began sobbing, unable to speak. It was some time before they were able to hear his horrific story.

Leo borrowed his father's van and drove to Carla's house. He told them all he knew of the terrible events in Baena. They had heard a little about the siege, but knew nothing of the massacres. Leo stayed with them for a while before returning to his parents' farm.

After Rosa had gone to sleep, José and Carla sat together and talked about the dangers and difficulties they were facing. José felt Carla was slipping into a depression. Her face was deathly white, her shoulders hunched and her head bent forward.

José tried to console her . They went to bed. He held her close and tried to make love to her but, in truth, neither really felt like it. They both lay still, listening for the slightest noise of danger outside.

He would have to keep a close watch on Carla and Rosa in future. He couldn't protect them from aggressive soldiers. Thankfully, they were in an isolated location. How could they escape from this madness?

Carla was in no fit state to travel through a war-torn country and anyhow, where could they go and how?

*

During the following days, there was much work to be done for the grape harvest. Nights were long and depressing, wishing for some solution to deliver them from their nightmare and waiting for soldiers to appear.

Carla's parents were in a similarly isolated farm and hoped that, by venturing out as little as possible, they would be safe. Vicente's delivery runs had to stop for a while, so money would be even tighter than normal.

José's parents' estate was in a prominent position in a wealthy area of wine estates. The harvests in the other bigger estates were going to suffer because many of their workers had been killed in Baena, or simply had not come back. More fortunately, Eduardo hadn't lost many of his workers and therefore his harvest promised to be reasonable.

Eduardo felt they had reason to believe they could escape the wrath of the military aggressors because many of the wine federation members were Falangists or just pro Nationalist. He hoped it would work out in their favour!

For a week, Baena seemed safe and then the Republican Militia came from Jaén, consolidated outside the town, and attacked Baena.

However, the following morning, the Nationalists counter attacked and the Republicans were forced to retreat from Baena, leaving the Nationalists still in control.

It was difficult to tell the difference between propaganda and truth. One Córdoba Nationalist newspaper reported that Nationalist forces caught armed murderers and, in line with military orders, dealt with them relentlessly. A Republican newspaper claimed that 1,200 were shot, their bodies stacked in the cemetery and burned. It seemed that both sides had taken and killed hostages, but numbers were often exaggerated.

3. PAIS BASCO (SPANISH BASQUE REGION) AND FINISTÈRE (BRITTANY)

Further North, were the Alonsos and Tanets

The Alonsos

Their story begins on Spain's northern coast, (Pais Basco), in Hondarribia, next to the French border, where the Alonso family owned a boat and fished, mainly for sardines.

Matias is the boat's Skipper and his wife, Maria, runs their home as a boarding house to supplement their income.

They have two sons, who crew and maintain the boat with their father. Louis, now a 22-year-old and Alan, a 21-year-old.

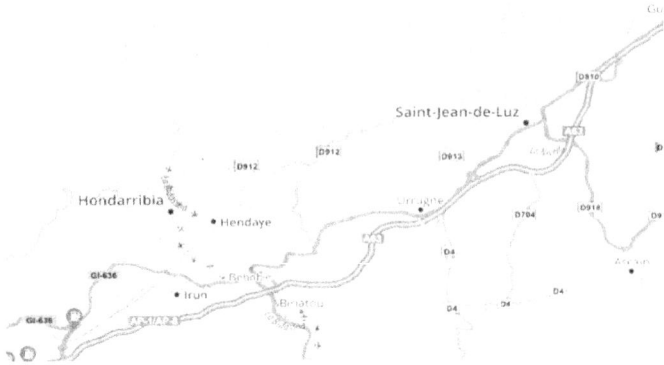

And the Tanets…

In Brittany, the brothers Corentin and Maugan, inherited an old fishing boat from their father. Corentin and his nephew, Josse, exchanged the old boat for a larger, more modern vessel with a big diesel engine, and, although they owned equal shares, Corentin was the skipper.

Mavis, (Corentin's wife), had two children. Lena, was now 19, she helped her mother on the family farm and assisted in maintaining the fishing nets. Paul, was now 18, he crewed in the boat, under the close supervision of his father.

Josse, (Maugan and Enora's son), was now 25. He inherited his father's share in the boat, when Maugan died.

The Alonsos all spoke Basque, but because they used to live across the border, in Saint Jean de Luz, they also spoke French better than Spanish. In addition, when the children were at school, they had a few elementary English lessons.

With the Civil War beginning on 17th July 1936, Franco's Nationalist forces advanced rapidly through the country. Matias and Maria were deeply concerned for the safety of their family, so they decided to rent out their house to a friend, load the boat with most of their possessions and head for Brittany. They had heard that Concarneau was an important Breton fishing port and it seemed like a good place where they should fit in easily, away from the Civil War.

They left on Tuesday, 4th August 1936, in the early hours of the morning, having anticipated a two-stage trip. The first stage to Les Sables d'Olonne would take an estimated 34 hours, based upon an average speed of 6 knots for an estimated 204 nautical miles.

Matias organised them into two pairs, taking 4-hour watches. Matias and Alan would take the first watch. When Matias and Alan took their second watch, they were in the deep waters of the Bay of Biscay and could feel the swell which continued during the night, but the weather was reasonable.

There were several uneventful sightings of other vessels … fishing boats, Spanish merchant ships and even a German warship.

The following afternoon, they arrived in the port of Les Sables d'Olonne. Maria and Alan yelled out in delight and relief.

Matias calmed them with, *"Steady, we still have another 27 hours or so at sea, before we reach Concarneau!"*

Maria looked at Alan, *"How can they live their lives like this, and tell us they enjoy it?"* Matias and Louis quietly grinned at each other.

Although the tourist season was at its height, they managed to find acceptable accommodation for the night, then joined the tourists in a friendly restaurant. After looking around the harbour, they returned to the hotel for a well-earned sleep.

They lingered over breakfast before heading out to sea again, for the final stage of their voyage to Concarneau.

After a misty night, rain welcomed them to Brittany's coastline.

Several fishing boats, heading out to sea, greeted

them noisily and they responded accordingly.

About midday, on Friday 7th August, they sighted the lighthouse on the Île Penfret, Conarneau's approach marker.

The rain stopped as they moored up in the harbour and Matias instructed, *"Stay on the boat while I sort out any paperwork."*

About half an hour later, he returned with a bottle of cider in each hand. *"We'll stay here for a few weeks, but, right now, we are going over there for a good meal."*

Later, they managed to book two rooms in a boarding house, for three weeks, until Friday 28th August, hoping to find a more permanent solution, while there.

The owner told them that the Fête des Filets Bleu was to be held on Saturday 22nd August. The festival would start in the evening and last the whole night.

He told them proudly, *"The town will be filled with tourists that weekend and the hostal will be full until the end of the month."*

He explained, *"The fête is named after the blue nets used by the Concarneau fishermen. The town, and the boats, will be decorated with coloured lights.*

"To the accompaniment of choirs, the fête queen and her maids of honour will arrive in a boat and be presented to the mayor.

"She will then lead a procession of horsemen, folk groups and fishermen's decorated carriages, to the walled city. The fête will finish with a fireworks display."

"Thank you," replied Maria, *"fantastic, we have arrived just in time!"* That night, the four of them went

to bed early and slept like logs!

*

In Audierne, like so many families involved in fishing and farming, especially in their region of Finistère, life was hard and the work left little time to spare.

Corentin skippered the boat, with his nephew, Josse, as first mate. Paul, Corentin's son, and four other experienced fishermen crewed, while fishing mainly for sardines and mackerel.

Mavis, Corentin's wife, managed their house and smallholding, which included chickens, a few pigs and a significant vegetable garden. Attached to the smallholding was a field which was currently planted with potatoes.

Lena assisted her mother, being principally responsible for the vegetable garden and the field. In addition, Lena helped Enora, Josse's mother, to maintain the fishing nets.

*

Unfortunately, in January 1936, Enora caught a cold and was coughing excessively. Then, sadly, in February, she died of pleurisy. This left Josse on his own in the cottage.

Corentin and Mavis told Josse that the loft in the farmhouse could easily be converted for him, but Josse declined, saying he preferred his independence and liked being close to the harbour.

With the loss of Enora, the crew now had to work with Lena to maintain the nets.

On Saturday, the 8th August, Corentin, Josse and Paul took the boat from Audierne, and headed for Concarneau to buy some new fishing gear.

Over lunch, they were introduced to Matias and Maria, who were hungry for knowledge of smaller ports and general advice to help them settle permanently. Matias and Maria were very interested in Corentin's description of the Tanet family's life and of Audierne as a fishing village.

Louis and Alan joined them a little later, explaining that they had been exploring the town. Josse welcomed the two young fellow fishermen.

Josse explained that, since his mother died, in February, he has been living alone in a three-bedroomed cottage by the harbour.

He invited the Alonso family to come and stay there with him.

*

"My uncle Corentin has offered to accommodate me in his house, if I want, so your family could stay in my house."

Corentin added, *"Why don't you bring your boat to Audierne ... I can organise a berth for it, (cheaper than here!), and you can stay temporarily in Josse's house.*

"If you retain your booking in the hostal, you can come back in your boat to Concarneau before the fête and still keep your options open for Josse's house. That way, you should enjoy the fête better.

"Our family will be coming here for the day and you can tell us then, what you want to do."

Matias looked at Maria, who nodded, *"Thank you both. We'd like that ... It sounds wonderful!"*

Corentin got up from the table, inclined his head towards Josse and Paul.

He said, *"Give us a few of days. Let's say on Thursday, bring your boat to Audierne... It'll probably take about five hours... and we'll look out for you about three o'clock."*

On their way home, Josse told Corentin that one of his friends in Concarneau had heard on the radio that France had just closed its Spanish border, declaring a 'non-intervention policy'.

As they approached Audierne, Corentin said, *"That was kind of you to offer your cottage to the Alonso family."*

Josse simply shrugged.

As agreed, the Alonsos arrived in Audierne harbour on the afternoon of Thursday 13th August, to be welcomed by the complete Tanet family.

After mooring the boat in their new berth, the Alonsos followed the Tanets to Josse's cottage and the visitors were shown around. His aunt Mavis had laid the table with a selection of aperitifs.

There were delighted smiles of acceptance all round when Maria said the cottage would be perfect for them and that she would leave the details to Matias and Josse.

"I'm looking forward to the company," replied Josse,

The five young folk took a drink and some food outside and popped in and out for more food.

Josse and Louis shared fishing stories, like old friends, while their younger siblings were more animated, asking questions about life in Audierne and Hondarribia. Alan, with his gentle inquisitive manner, was constantly drawn to the slim, petite, 19-year-old Lena, with her engaging smile and dark brown eyes. She, in turn, liked the attention from the slim tanned handsome young man. Lena's brother, Paul, probed Alan about life in the south and Lena and Paul were careful to include him in getting to know one another.

While the young folks were outside, Matias thanked Corentin again and told him they had kept the booking in the hostal, but informed the owner they would be in Audierne for some of the time.

Later, Corentin, Mavis, Lena and Paul, made their way home, leaving the others to sort themselves out.

In the cottage, Josse invited Matias and Maria to use the bedroom which was his parent's room. Josse showed Louis and Alan into another room.

"This was my bedroom, but I will use the small room next-door and move some of my junk into the bed-recess in the living room."

The brothers thanked him very much, but he responded with, *"No problem, the house will be a family home again!"*

The Alonsos settled into the cottage without delay. There was a mutual acceptance between Maria and Josse, that he would be treated as another son.

Mavis and Maria soon became friends and agreed that Alan's keen interest in Lena, was being reciprocated, albeit with apparent shyness in front of others.

Matias accepted an invitation from Corentin to go fishing the following Monday, returning on Wednesday. Then, on Thursday, the Alonsos went in their own boat to Concarneau, ready for Saturday's fête.

As dawn broke on the Saturday, the Tanets boat left Audierne, and arrived in Concarneau in time to meet the Alonsos for lunch.

Although the hostal owner had told his guests what to look for, the pageant exceeded everybody's expectations and the two families became firm friends. After the fireworks finale, the Alonsos retired to the hostal, Mavis, Corentin and Lena spent the rest of the night with some relations, and Josse and Paul slept on the boat.

The Tanets returned to Audierne on Sunday 23rd and the Alonsos followed on Friday 28th August, 1936.

The two families in Audierne

In September, Corentin reorganised his boat crew, with Josse, (aged 25) as first mate, Paul, (aged 18) and three of the original crew.

Matias now had Louis (aged 22) as his first mate, Alan (aged 21), plus one crew member transferred from Corentin and two new 18-year-olds with limited experience.

In addition, Corentin and Matias agreed to take on Max, a friend of Josse, and an experienced fisherman, who wanted to leave a smaller sailing boat.

Max joined as a carpenter and maintenance man, but

also, to be available as a relief crew member for either boat. Lena would continue to help maintaining the fishing nets.

The two boats often sailed out together and fished within sight of each other ... It seemed to work well, and added a measure of safety, in case of difficulty. It also produced friendly competition and banter between the two crews.

On Sundays, when the weather was reasonable, Alan would walk to the family farm to help Lena in the vegetable garden or the field. The two families spent Christmas day 1936 together at the farm, with Mavis and Maria putting on a variety of Breton and Spanish dishes.

In the afternoon, after dinner, Lena and Alan stole a few moments in a quiet spot and Lena cuddled close to Alan, saying, *"This is lovely! I miss you when you are at sea!"*

Before they could embrace, Mavis interrupted, *"Ah there you are! ... Lena, come and help in the kitchen!"*

Lena scowled, but followed. Alan shrugged and went to see what the others were up to.

Escalation of the War in 1936

The radio announced that German and Italian planes had brought more troops from Morocco to Cádiz, that Sevilla was in Nationalist hands and, later, they took Badajoz, murdering thousands of Republicans in the Bull Ring.

Mass systematic rape of women was reportedly

approved by the Nationalist General Queipo de Llano.

A Republican offensive failed to oust the Nationalists from Córdoba city. After a two-month siege of Toledo, Nationalists murdered hundreds of hostages.

By November, a large Nationalist army reached the Madrid suburbs. The International Brigade joined the Republican defence. One thousand Nationalists were murdered by Republican Guards. By the end of the month, the battle for Madrid had reached a stalemate.

In December, the Nationalists, in increased numbers, advanced eastwards from Córdoba towards Andujar, (north of Baena). Then Republicans, including the International Brigade, launched a counteroffensive. but were decimated at Villa del Rio and again at Lopera. By end of 1936, the Nationalist army reached Porcuna but failed to take Andújar.

In Audierne, 1937 began with storms which prevented the boats from going out. Mavis lectured Corentin, *"Instead of getting in my way, why don't you work in the attic? For years, you have been promising to make it into a bedroom!"*

On Sunday 28th February, the families gathered at the cottage to celebrate Lena's 20th birthday.

Her birthday wasn't until the following Tuesday, but the boats were going out the next day and wouldn't return until the day after her birthday.

Maria confided in Mavis, *"It's clear that Alan and Lena are becoming closer and closer. I don't think it will be long before the two of them start talking about marriage. You know, I was only her age when Matias and I were married. I feel happy for them. What do you think?"*

Mavis replied quietly, "He's almost 22 now, but I don't think he is quiet ready. I have asked Corentin to convert our attic into a bedroom, and see what develops!"

"That's a good idea. Let me know if there is anything I can do to help!"

Mavis kept up the pressure on Corentin and on Saturday, 27th March, the day before Easter, Mavis and Lena quietly finished decorating the attic.

Then, on Easter Sunday, Mavis and Lena proudly showed Alan the final result. She knew she had struck a chord there, although she made it clear that it was not to be used as a love nest.

When Lena and Alan stole a few moments alone, Alan looked around. *"There's enough room here for a double bed!"*

Lena blushed and whispered guiltily, *"I know!"*

Each time Matias and Maria heard news of the Civil War in Spain, they were relieved to have moved to Brittany, but worried for friends they had left behind.

At the end of April, they heard the worst imaginable news.

*

On the afternoon of 26th April, 1937, the market town of Guernica, near Bilbao, was bombed to destruction on a market day, when there were usually about 10,000 people in the town.

For over three hours the town suffered carpet

bombing from about fifty German and Italian bombers and fighters ... The bombers obliterated most of the buildings in the town and the fighters machine-gunned people running from the scene of devastation ...

Accurate reports and propaganda of deaths varied from a couple of hundred to one thousand six hundred, plus an unspecified number of wounded ... For the next three days, fires continued to burn, adding further problems for rescuers.

In those days, in April 1937, the horror of Guernica was etched into Basque hearts and into Spanish history for the world to remember.

Maria sobbed, *"That's not far from where we lived! War is terrible. Where's the triumph and glory in such a massacre?"*

Louis and Alan cursed the *'German and Italian Fascist warmongers'*. Matias warned them against any ideas of returning to Spain and fighting against Fascism.

Then, in May, 4,000 Basque children were evacuated on SS *Habana* and taken to Southampton from where, homes were found for them in England and Wales. Before the onset of winter in 1937, northern Spain had fallen to Franco's Nationalist army.

Increasingly, the spread of Fascism was threatening the rest of Europe. The Nationalist Party in Brittany, (the PNB), with their pro-Nazi philosophy, gained a political toehold. The majority of Bretons and the national government were being pushed to the limit and a crackdown on extremists began.

The year had become progressively gloomier, and

even Christmas had lost some of its sparkle. However, the families' spirits were lifted when Alan and Lena announced their engagement to be married the following year.

4. ANDALUCÍA

A Dangerous Survival Plan in Baena

Carla's uncontrollable fear of being surrounded and attacked by brutal Nationalist forces was inconsolable and every loud noise added to her severe depression. How could José protect Rosa and Carla? The danger was becoming closer and closer.

Leo made many visits to Carla, José and Rosa, for mutual updates. Also, José took the back roads on his motorbike to visit his parents. With these visits, plus radio and newspaper propaganda, augmented by local gossip, the families kept reasonably up to date with the events of the Civil War.

At the beginning of January 1937, their understanding of the war was that Malaga, and then Almería would soon fall to the Nationalist army. Tens of thousands were dying in Madrid and the Basque Country whilst the Republicans still retained control of Cataluña, Valencia and Murcia

Portugal was helping Franco. France was unpredictable. The Germans and Italians were blockading the coast, while the British navy respected a non-proliferation agreement and simply looked on. The International Brigades were based in Albacete and somehow they were managing to enter and leave Spain.

Early in January 1937, José, Carla and Leo sat round the table and José began, *"Leo, I've been struggling to work out a plan which will give us our best chance for the future. Carla and I are in agreement with what I am about to say.*

"We don't want Rosa to be here with the proverbial sword of Damocles over her head for the rest of her life (which could end violently) ...

"If Carla and I try to go with her to another country, I think Carla would be seriously at risk from soldiers who have been told by their commander that they can freely rape women. Also I don't think she is strong enough for the long journey. Therefore, I have to stay here and look after Carla.

"Our parents should also stay here. So ... if Rosa is to escape, we think that only YOU could take her away from this engulfing terror! PLEASE think about it and if you agree, we need to work out a plan before the advancing army cuts us off completely."

"My God!" said Leo and a long silence followed.

Then José continued, *"You should go home and think about it, maybe we should talk it over with our parents!"*

After a further long silence, Leo gave his decision.

"If I have to go and talk this through with our parents, then I am the wrong man for the job. My answer is YES. It may be dangerous, but probably the best for Rosa. I will continue to love her, but also be her guardian. I will do everything I can to take her to safety!"

"Thank you!" replied José and Carla, with sombre expressions.

They talked well into the early hours until Leo said that he'd better go home because his parents would be worrying if something had happened to him.

Before he left, Carla suggested that he should come and stay with them. Time was pressing and they needed every available minute to plan the details.

"Agreed," replied Leo *"See you tomorrow!"*

*

After the door closed, Carla looked at José. *"I hope we're doing the right thing ... We may never see her again!"*

"I know, darling, we love her dearly but know it's her best chance. Leo will look after her and make it happen if anyone can."

Early the following morning, José rode over to tell his parents of the plan.

They said José and family could come and live there, but it wouldn't really be any safer. They said how Rosa would be missed and how she was worried for Rosa and Leo's safety.

It seemed to her like another one of José's daring schemes. However, they would all have to make the most of it.

His father asked if there was any way he could help. José thanked him but declined and said he had to get back home quickly.

As he left, his mother shouted, *"Give Carla and Rosa our love ... and tell Leo that he and Rosa will be in our prayers."*

Not long after José returned home to Carla and Rosa, Vicente and Teresa brought Leo, (and his few possessions). A long discussion followed.

Vicente was two characters in one … When he was in the fields, in his well-worn clothes and battered hat, he was part of the countryside around him. The goats and the dogs changed, but not Vicente.

At home, he was someone else. When he took off his boots and walked into Teresa's world, he hung up his other personality on the peg before washing, shaving and changing his clothes. Not until then was he rewarded with loving hugs and kisses from Teresa.

Today, he was simply a loving supportive father and grandfather.

Teresa almost changed Carla's mind and the two of them clung to each other, sobbing sniffling and looking at Rosa who wanted to know what was going on.

José explained, *"It's the war, precious, we have to talk about something complicated."*

Rosa huffed, *"When you talk about the war, you always say it's complicated, and then get sad."* She went outside and played in her tiny house of logs.

Vicente thought it might be better if they waited for warmer weather, but he agreed that many of the soldiers in Andalucía were extremists from the Moroccan campaign and they were too close.

Maybe this plan, with Leo's help, could save their granddaughter and, of course, their son. Eventually, they all agreed on the plan and many different thoughts were voiced … some useful, some not, but all had a hearing.

One of the suggestions voiced by Vicente was that they should sign a paper to agree to the adoption of Rosa by Leo but none of them wanted to go to Baena to ask a notary to draw up official papers. Instead, José wrote out a declaration of adoption which was signed by each one of them, stating their relationship to Rosa.

José handed the completed document to Leo saying, *"As you have seen, this document states that we have faith in you to be a good guardian and parent to Rosa … We already know that, but this will tell others, of our trust in you."*

Leo took it solemnly and put it in his wallet.

They agreed that Valencia seemed like a reasonable place to head for, since it was now the seat of the Republican government. Also, since Albacete was in that direction and the International Brigade was based there, maybe they could get help from them … Obviously they had links outside Spain.

Teresa said, *"My sister and husband, (Begoña and Felipe Ortega), have a smallholding near Jaen. Vicente, you could take Leo and Rosa there*

"The rebels haven't got that far yet. It's on the way to Albacete isn't it?"

Leo said, *"Will you do that, Papa?"*

Vicente agreed. *"It's your move now, son!"*

Rosa came in, *"Are you happy yet? I'm hungry!"*

Over a meal, they gradually told Rosa that bad men were attacking homes in the town and that they wanted to take her to a safe place far away. But Mama was very sick and couldn't travel, so Papa had to stay at home and look after her. They explained to Rosa that they loved her very much but she had to accept Leo as her new Papa and he was going to take her on a long journey to safety.

"When will I come back home?" she asked hesitantly.

"Maybe after the war, darling, but we don't know. It could be a very long time.That's why Uncle Leo will look after you and be your new Papa."

After the meal, Vicente and Teresa said it was time for them to go home and as they got into the van, Leo said, *"Papa, would you please come back tomorrow and help me finalise the plan?"*

Vicente agreed, closed the van door and drove away.

Once Rosa was in bed, Leo and José bounced ideas off one another to help prepare Leo for what lay ahead. Carla gave Leo more advice on how best to deal with Rosa. They weren't sure whether or not Leo should be armed, but the only guns the family had were old shotguns which were far too cumbersome and couldn't be hidden easily. So there wasn't really a choice, and anyway, Leo didn't want to be seen as some kind of militia man. However, he would take his hunting knife, in its sheath.

He would have to limit their luggage to a large haversack and double bedroll for him and a small satchel for Rosa. On his chest, he would carry a small food and drink haversack which would be slung round his neck. This arrangement would leave his hands free and Rosa could feel she had something personal, but not heavy.

The next morning, they organised their clothing, trying to balance the need to keep out the cold and rain of winter in the north, but allowing for the following summer, because they didn't know how long this journey would take.

When Vicente arrived, he was surprised to see that they were ready for him to take them to his place and they would start the big journey from there. For Rosa's sake, Leo wanted the minimum of fuss and after brooding over a cup of coffee, they reminded themselves that, last night, they agreed a happy farewell was necessary … Vicente went to the van while the others kissed and hugged their goodbyes.

Carla tried to look cheerful. *"You and Uncle Leo need to look after each other. Remember, he's now your new Papa and it's OK to call him Papa. Love each other and keep each other happy. Go with God!"*

Laughing and joking, Leo took Rosa's hand, as they climbed into the van beside Vicente.

With a final wave, Vicente crunched the gears and they slowly drove away. With forced smiles and tearful eyes, José and Carla watched the van until they could see it no longer. Only then, did they go into the house and stand forlornly in each other's arms until José helped Carla into a chair and he slumped into another. They both sat there silently, staring into a fog of despair. They would have to be strong!

Preparing to Leave Baena...

Teresa heard Vicente's van arrive.

She looked sadly at Rosa and Leo when they came into the living room and put their travel things in a corner. Leo said, *"Come on Rosa, let's go and play with Granddad's dog ... What's his name?"*

"Pepe!" chirped Rosa, looking up at Leo with a happy smile.

Teresa went up to the attic to make up a bed for Rosa, beside Leo's bed. After that, she went back to the kitchen to continue cooking lunch and baking two farmhouse loaves, for the journey to Jaén.

Ana and Miguel were looking after the goats. Vicente busied himself checking the van for tomorrow's journey to Jaén. The family, including Ana and Miguel, had a hearty lunch of vegetable stew with chorizo, followed by rice pudding.

Throughout the afternoon and evening, they talked about many things, but naturally the main topics were, Jaén, Aunt Begoña and Uncle Felipe Ortega and the long journey beyond Jaén.

In the morning, Teresa insisted that they eat a good breakfast and Vicente put some cheeses, milk, bread and anís into the van.

Leo put their bags into the van's cabin and announced that they were ready to go. Miguel hoped he would have a good journey and returned to his work in the milking parlour.

Ana gave Leo several kisses and while holding him tightly, she said, *"I will miss you. You made me part of your family and I love you for it. I don't want you to leave but wish you Good Luck, my darling!"*

Teresa couldn't hold back her tears while kissing and hugging Leo and Rosa, *"Have a safe journey, my dears!"*

It was Saturday 30th January 1937 ... Their journey had begun!

First Refuge near Jaén

Vicente had heard that there were large numbers of Nationalist troops coming from Córdoba and going South East, in the direction of Granada.

Normally, he would use that road for almost twenty kilometres and, before Alcaudete, turn off for Jaén.

Today however, he proposed to cross the Granada road earlier, take smaller roads north for about twenty kilometres and approach Martos from the west. From there, they would go onto the main Baena/Jaén road for the remaining part of the journey.

Whilst still in the nearby outskirts of Luque, Vicente confirmed they were on the right road. They soon came to the Granada road and, sure enough, there was a military convoy heading for Granada. They waited until it had gone, quickly crossed over and kept on the smaller road.

*

It was about 11 o'clock, they agreed that a coffee would be welcome, but decided it would be better to press on, especially since Rosa had fallen asleep. At about midday, Vicente pointed out that Martos was just ahead of them and it was time to stop for a drink and a bite to eat.

Although Rosa declared that she was hungry, she had eaten enough after a few bites of bread and cheese and a gulp of milk. The three of them walked up and down for a few minutes, then, one by one, they satisfied their toilet needs and climbed back into the van.

Less than an hour later, not far from Jaén, they turned off the main road near Torre Del Campo and soon arrived at Begoña and Felipe's smallholding. Their property was close to the Via Verde railway line, which, before the Civil War, had been used to carry olive oil from Luque to Jaén.

In those days, most people didn't have telephones, so

Teresa had been unable to ask if her sister if Leo and Rosa could have their first refuge with them in Jaén, before continuing on their long journey.

When the van drew up in their yard, Begoña and Felipe were having a siesta. They sleepily looked into the yard to see who had arrived.

Naturally, they were not only surprised but also worried, especially when her sister, Teresa, wasn't there too.

The surprise visitors were welcomed. The reason for their visit was given at length by Leo, with supporting interventions from Vicente.

Begoña was shocked, but looked sympathetically at Rosa and said what a lovely surprise it was to see her, and she brought Leo too!

Felipe assured them, *"You can both stay here as long as you like. Francisco's room is free. Our son is now a sergeant in the navy, serving on the destroyer* Lepanto.*"*

Vicente and Leo went out to the van and brought in the cheeses, milk, bread and anis, which were all loudly appreciated.

Vicente said he should leave right away because he wanted to get back home before dark, and anyway, Teresa would be worrying.

"Will you be alright Dad, it's a long drive home on your own?"

"Of course son, I'm used to doing my rounds on my own!"

They wished him a safe journey home and Vicente left without any more fuss.

His journey home was uneventful and, during the evening meal, he sat with Teresa, Ana and Miguel, trying to make it sound as though life at the farm would be almost back to normal, although they knew it would never be the same again! At least Leo and Rosa would be safe with Begoña and Felipe!

In Jaen, Felipe was struggling to find out how he could help Leo and Rosa to move closer to Albacete, until he thought about his old friend Manuel ... For many years, until last summer, Felipe used to see his best friend, Manuel Herrera, every Friday at their favourite bar.

However, Manuel now lived in Úbeda, where he managed the garage of the local hospital ... *It's worth a try*, thought Felipe.

After several calls from a public phone shop, he got through to Manuel in the garage at Úbeda hospital and made arrangements for the two pals to meet again. Also, Manuel didn't mind if Felipe brought his nephew with him.

He wanted Leo to introduce himself, explain the circumstances and see if Manuel could provide the next staging post in their travels.

Begoña and Leo showered Rosa with lots of love and gently encouraged her to call Leo 'Papa'. Begoña told childhood stories of her and her sister, (Rosa's grandma Teresa).

Leo's full name was Leo García Díaz, (García being his father's family name and Díaz being his mother's family name): Rosa's full name was Rosa Sánchez

García, (Sánchez being her father's family name and García being her mother's family name).

In order to help Rosa to be recognised as Leo's daughter, Leo dropped his mother's name and Rosa would drop her father's name, so that they became simply Leo and Rosa García.

The following week, they met Manuel in Úbeda and he took them to see his wife who was charmed by Leo and sympathetic to his task. Because Úbeda is more into the mountains and tends to be colder than Jaén and Torre Del Campo, it was agreed that Felipe shouldn't bring Leo and Rosa until March 1937.

*

On the day when Leo was away, Rosa became more and more nervous and restless. She hadn't seen her Mummy and Daddy for a long time, and now Uncle Leo, who was supposed to be her new papa, had left her.

The kind lady was her Grandma's sister, but this wasn't Rosa's home. She wanted her Mummy, and her Grandma and she missed Granddad's dog, Pepe.

Begoña did her best to keep the five-year-old busy, feeding the chickens and collecting eggs, helping with baking bread and finally, when Leo and Felipe returned, Rosa was asleep on Begoña's lap.

Leo picked her up gently and as he sat down with her on his lap, she woke up and put her little arms round him (as far as they would go!)

"Why did you leave me? Was I naughty? When are Mummy and Daddy coming?"

Leo spoke softly to her, *"Remember, there are a lot of people fighting each other and doing bad things ... Mummy and Daddy wanted to come with you, away from where they live and where Grandma and Granddad live ... but Mummy isn't as strong as we are, so she couldn't come. Daddy had to stay with her and I promised to look after you and take you somewhere safe. Today, I went with Uncle Felipe to see some friends who will give us another safe place to stay on this journey of ours ... I should have taken you with me ... I'm sorry!"*

Those big sad green eyes penetrated his soul, *"Don't leave me again!"*

"No I won't, Rosa darling!" promised Leo.

While they were living at Felipe and Begoña's smallholding, Leo helped to rebuild a crumbling old barn attached to the house and occasionally, he and Rosa would go with Felipe in his pick-up truck to fetch cement from a factory which was only about five minutes away. When they were out, Felipe warned that the Nationalist army had taken Porcuna, about fifteen minutes' drive north-west of where they bought the cement.

Most evenings, they would sit around the log fire and talk or listen to the radio, while Felipe smoked his pipe and Begoña sewed, but sometimes Felipe would read and Leo would play dominoes or cards with Rosa.

One day, they walked into the village of Torre Del Campo, with the promise that they would find something for Rosa.

Although it meant a lot of walking for her, the thought of looking for something, just for her, kept her going.

They looked around in the town and found what Leo was looking for. A shop which sold children's story books and the clear favourite was a book containing illustrated stories of Sleeping Beauty, Cinderella, Snow White and others.

On their return, after dinner, in the warm glow from the fire, Rosa looked at Leo with her big eyes, *"Papa, will you read to me from this book every night, before I go to sleep?"*

Leo gently corrected her, *"We are going to read it together!"* (And, of course, that's what they did, nearly every night for several years to come!)

They learned from the radio that Málaga had been attacked by a large force of Moors, Nationalists and Italians troops, while the Republicans held 600 prisoners hostage in a prison ship, shooting batches of them in reprisals for air raids … Early in February, they finally surrendered to the Nationalists …

The battle for Madrid was raging on and the Basque and Catalan regions were also suffering badly from the war.

The subsequent massive exodus of refugees along the coast road to Almería was subjected to air raids and shelling from the sea … Franco's soldiers in Málaga killed large numbers of prisoners and, conducted mass raping of women, in accordance with their orders to create terror among the population, but the Italian authorities were horrified at the inhumanity of the Nationalist forces.

The Republican navy had to relinquish its Málaga

base and retreat, eastwards, to Almería and Cartagena. Thankfully, Felipe and Begoña's son was still alive on board the *Lepanto*.

5. AUDIERNE

In late February 1938, Paul was pleased to be accepted, at last, as a permanent crew member on the Tanet boat. Alan, on the other hand, although happy being a crew member on the Alonso boat, wanted to learn farming, so he could be with Lena.

Everybody was happy with the new way of working.

Mavis enjoyed guiding Alan and Lena, and felt less pressure as Alan's enthusiasm and knowledge of farming increased.

Alan and Lena developed a new respect for one another, which gave them confidence while planning their wedding.

In May, their parents gave the couple a present of a new double bed, complete with fine bedding accessories. Other presents included cutlery, glasses and a variety of household things.

The wedding was a joyous relief from the depressing news from Spain and Germany.

For their honeymoon, they stayed for two nights in Douarnenez, another fishing port nearby, and then two nights in Quimper, the capital of Finistère. On their return, they worked tirelessly on the farm and Lena helped Mavis prepare meals for the family. At last, Mavis had some free time!

Unfortunately, the depressing news from Spain continued and by the end of the year, Franco had won all of Spain, except Madrid.

It now looked like the Republicans would soon surrender to him.

6. ANDALUCÍA

Second Refuge in Úbeda

It was March 1937.

Leo and Rosa had become part of Begoña and Felipe's family, but, as agreed, it was time to move on, so they packed their things and said emotional farewells as they settled into Felipe's pick-up.

About an hour later, near Baeza, as the road started to climb, they could feel the temperature drop slightly and snow could be seen on the distant mountains to their right.

After another half hour or so, on entering Úbeda, Felipe pointed out the Hospital de Santiago on their left and the Plaza de Toros on their right. They turned into one side street and then another before stopping outside the house of Manuel and Carmen Herrera.

The house was a very old whitewashed three-storey town house with a heavy panelled oak door which had been freshly varnished. Rosa held Leo's hand as he rang the doorbell.

A window opened above them. *"Just a moment, I'll let you in,"* shouted Carmen. Then, the door was opened by a sallow faced slim little lady wearing a housecoat. Carmen gave them a wrinkly smile …

"So this is the lovely Rosa. You are all welcome. Come in, Manuel is at work, he won't be home until this evening ... I've been looking forward to seeing you, especially you, Rosa, I've made some pastries. Do you like pastries Rosa? Come; let's go to the kitchen."

She held out her hand to Rosa, who gave her a shy smile, looked up at Leo and held his hand tighter.

"It's OK!" assured Leo. *"We are going to be happy here, I know it!"*

Felipe brought in a large box of vegetables and eggs which pleased Carmen and they sat round the table to tuck into pastries like the ones Ana used to give them ... Carmen chatted incessantly. *"Just like my mother,"* thought Leo.

Felipe said he couldn't wait for Manuel because Begoña was expecting him to be home for lunch. Carmen suggested that he should come with Begoña in a fortnight's time, after Semana Santa, (Easter week), and they agreed the details before Felipe left.

7. THE SOLDIER

Andrew Banks was a soldier in the No.1 Company of the International Brigade's Marseillaise Battalion. The previous Christmas Day, they were trying to capture the town of Lopera, (north-west of Jaén).

Andrew, an Englishman from Peterborough, was a short, brown-haired loquacious young man with hazel eyes and bushy eyebrows. At the age of 24, he was recruited in Paris, near the Sorbonne, where he was a second-year student studying French and Spanish.

It wasn't long before he was on a train, crossing the border into Spain, bound for Albacete, the Brigade's headquarters and training camp. Once there, he joined the newly formed Number One Company of the Marseillaise Battalion and was issued with an ex-British First World War uniform and an old Lee-Enfield .303 rifle. The company comprised of about a hundred and forty English speaking soldiers, mostly without any previous military experience. They were given very little training before being sent to the front at Lopera.

From 27th to 29th December 1936, the Marseillaise Battalion bravely fought against forces which were superior in numbers, experience and equipment.

They suffered heavy casualties from machine guns, mortars, artillery and even air attacks. After advancing, retreating and advancing again, the companies lost communication with their commanders, became disorganised and finally withdrew in chaos ... many exhausted, without ammunition and hadn't eaten all day.

Of the survivors who escaped the enemy, many of the injured failed to reach their units again for some time ... Many of those who could walk, simply stumbled vaguely away from the setting sun and the enemy in the west.

A few days later, their Battalion Commander was court-martialled for treason and shot.

Andrew had taken cover on the third day.

He was in a depression among olive trees when mortar shells were exploding around him ... He couldn't remember exactly what happened, except that he blacked out and when he came to, he was deaf and blind. His whole body was shaking, he had a tremendous pain in his head and his right hand was a useless bloody mess ...

As his hearing returned, he crawled away from the sound of gunfire, unable to see where he was going.

"You all right, mate?" came a voice immediately above him.

"Yea ... I've had too much wine and I'm out for a crawl," he replied.

"Sorry, it was a stupid question. Let me help you up . My God, your face is covered with blood and look at your hand! Hold on to me, I think Piccadilly is this way!"

Andrew put his hand to his forehead and felt warm blood above his right eye.

"Let's sit down here!" said the stranger, *"I've got a bandage, let's stop the bleeding and cover up your wounds."*

Gradually, through his left eye, Andrew made out a very hazy figure in a familiar uniform. *"I'm blind in this eye,"* as he indicated his right eye, *"and my vision in the other is hazy and comes and goes and my hand hurts like hell!"*

The pair of them stumbled on until they reached a tiny, isolated farmhouse. An attractive, generously proportioned woman came out of the house, saw that Andrew was wounded and as she and his rescuer helped him into the house, Andrew collapsed on the floor.

He was in bed when he woke up the following morning.

"Ah! My English soldier is awake!" said the woman as she came in from the living room.

"How did I get here?" he said while looking around the room and seeing only a cloudy picture.

*

He was aware of his nakedness, then focussed on the trousers and tunic draped over a chair and made a move towards them. *"Ouch!"* He touched his bandaged head and slumped back onto the bed. *"God, I don't know what hurts more ... my head or my hand!"*

The woman spoke in Spanish, but, of course, thanks to his studies in England and Paris, Andrew understood.

"That's a bad cut over your eye. While you were unconscious, I was able to clean it and remove a piece of metal. You've now got a fresh bandage on it. Both your

eyes are very red especially your right one. Your fingers have been seriously damaged and I've done what little I can with your hand!"

A little later, she helped Andrew to a sitting position and covered his back and shoulders with a blanket. She gave him a large cup and steadied it, while he used his left hand to hold it as he sipped sweet coffee.

"Where's the man who brought me here?"

"Oh he just stopped for a little food and drink before saying that you are in good hands, and then he left."

"I don't even know his name! and Señora, I don't know your name either!"

"My name is Pilar Rodriguez. My husband was a doctor in Andujar and I was a nurse. He became seriously ill and had to stop working. I nursed him here at home, but he died three years ago at the age of 44."

"So what's your name?"

"My name is Andrew Banks, but friends call me Andy."

"Pleased to meet you, Andy. My friends call me Pili! Now you stay there, while I wash your dirty uniform."

For several days, Pili nursed him as well as she could and vision in his left eye improved slightly, but he was still virtually blind in his right one and he suffered severe headaches. She was also worried about his hand. He desperately needed hospital treatment.

She thought for a while.

"I have neighbours, not far from here, who were patients of my husband for many years ... sometimes, I cycle over there and on occasions, they give me a lift to

Andujar and back."

"If they drive me to the medical centre where I used to work, maybe I could persuade one of the doctors to take you to hospital."

The next morning, with her neighbour's help, Pili made one of the doctors promise to help, and she returned home with the good news for Andy.

True to his word, the doctor knocked on Pili's door the following day. After examining Andy, he said that the hand needed urgent surgery, but eye treatment was more complicated and would have to wait. He bundled Andy into his car and took him to the medical centre where he called in one of his friends who was a retired surgeon.

*

That evening, they operated on Andy's hand and had to amputate the ends of all four fingers so that he lost his fingertips and adjacent knuckles.

The doctor then drove a heavily sedated Andy back to Pili's house where he knew that, in these troubled times, his patient would receive the nursing care he needed. Andy's hand would probably have turned gangrenous and could have led to his death if he hadn't had the surgery and Pili's subsequent devoted nursing care.

Pili put Andy to bed and after a few hours, he drifted in and out of consciousness. Pili moved in beside him and held him close. The bedroom shutters were closed and neither of them was aware of the arrival of the sun heralding a new day. Gradually, Andy responded to her tenderness and, tentatively, began to explore her naked body with his left hand.

Both his eyes were bandaged and it seemed to intensify his desire and overcome his pain. Their lips met and tongues probed each other's open mouth. Initially, their lovemaking was slow and gentle as though seeking each other's approval, but soon their full passion exploded.

She was a little older than Andy, but it was irrelevant and as the weeks went by, their affection for each other developed. She wanted him to get hospital treatment for his eyes. Her belief that Andy was suffering from glaucoma was supported by his frequent headaches and that he often lost his balance. Alternatively, she didn't want to lose her very dear companion and lover.

Andy had become so content in Pili's company that he too didn't want to leave, so the decision to leave was postponed although they both knew his departure was inevitable.

Eventually, they discussed where, how and when he should go.

Firstly, Pili insisted that he should go to hospital for better treatment to both his eyes and she thought Úbeda hospital was far enough away from the conflict and better placed than Jaen. Andy accepted that. Secondly, to travel, he should avoid contact with the military, who would probably try to give him a quick fix and put him back in action, (although it was difficult to imagine how!) ... and Andy accepted that.

Thirdly, the forthcoming Semana Santa, (Easter Holy Week), could cause something of a diversion, although

Palm Sunday should be avoided because it would be more difficult to get transport then.

"So Thursday 18th March would be a good day to aim for. Sounds good in theory" said Andy, *"But how?"*

Pili went to the medical centre again.

On her return, she explained that the doctor had agreed to her plan, and an ambulance should be able to come and collect Andy, but they had no idea when. However, her patient should not be wearing uniform, although it was recommended that he bring it in a suitcase.

Over a week later, Pili's doctor friend arrived in a car. He explained that it would be better if he took Andy to the clinic immediately, because an ambulance from Úbeda was due at the clinic, in about two hours' time, to collect a patient.

But also, he had spoken to a consultant he knew at Úbeda's Hospital de Santiago. Andy would be accepted as a patient.

Tearfully, Pili helped Andy into some of her husband's clothes. Andy packed his uniform into a battered old suitcase and she held him tightly while leading him to the car.

As they kissed, for the last time, Andy whispered, *"You have saved my life and given me a will to live!"*

"And you have done the same for me, my love."

At the medical centre, the doctor helped Andy into his consulting room and it wasn't long before the ambulance drew up and, holding his suitcase, Andy was stretchered into it. Shortly after, they stopped to pick up another stretchered patient who silently kept him company to the hospital.

Andy was formally admitted to the hospital, stating, as previously instructed, that he was a foreign worker on Pili's farm and that he had lost his papers at the time of his accident. The consultant came to see him and waived away bureaucratic questions from the staff.

"I will examine your hand tomorrow, but don't expect anything to be done to your eyes because we don't have any specialist eye surgeons here.

"You have been admitted as a civilian, so keep your military things in your suitcase in that locked cupboard and remember, our patients and staff include both Republicans and Nationalists, some of whom are extremists, but this is a hospital and any trouble will be dealt with immediately and harshly."

As promised, the consultant examined Andy's hand and said that further surgery was needed on his fingers, but it couldn't be done right away.

The next day, after several X-rays from their new machine the consultant said the injury to Andy's forehead did not contain any metal fragments and should heal, albeit leaving a scar. Sight in his left eye should hopefully improve a little, with further nursing care.

However, his right eye urgently needed a delicate operation from a highly experienced consultant and in Spain, maybe that could normally be done in Madrid, Barcelona or possibly in Valencia but he felt that, in these times of civil war, it would not be possible. It was thought that advances in eye surgery were currently being made in London's Eye Hospital, if only he could reach there!

On the Sunday after his arrival in the hospital, a nurse had just finished bathing his eyes when Andy heard the sound of many drums beating a slow march. *"What has happened?"* he asked the nurse.

"It's the march of one of the brotherhoods for Semana Santa," she replied.

"Oh, of course!" responded a relieved Andy. *"This week is Semana Santa ... I had lost all sense of time but why haven't I heard other celebrations?"*

The nurse shrugged her shoulders, *"It's the war, I suppose!"*

Meanwhile, for Leo and Rosa

On Friday, 2nd April 1937, in the house not far from the Hospital de Santiago, Leo had read to Rosa and kissed her goodnight ... He returned to the living room where Manuel and Carmen were listening to an evening news programme on the radio ... It was announced that the previous day, the German Condor Legion, on behalf of the Nationalists, had bombed Jaén.

At the beginning of the following week, Manuel was at work when he received a telephone call from Felipe, wanting to confirm that the following Saturday would be suitable for Begoña and him to visit.

Manuel said that he had heard about the bombing back in Jaén and asked if Begoña and Felipe had been affected by it. *"No, but we heard it. It seems that there were six Junkers bombers in a bunch. They bombed houses and killed over a hundred and fifty people … many places are in ruins. There was nothing to stop them since Jaén doesn't have any guns to fire back at them."*

"That's terrible," replied Manuel, *"but, yes … we look forward to seeing you both on Saturday."*

During the week, Andy's consultant brought his car into the garage to fix some minor problem and, while a mechanic was working on the car, the consultant and Manuel chatted. Manuel asked how the Englishman was doing and the consultant said it would be ideal if he could go back to London for an eye operation, but how would that be possible?

They were both aware of trucks going through Úbeda, taking stragglers from Lopera up to Albacete … But how could they persuade them to take their Englishman?

"Can I confide in you?" Said Manuel.

"But of course!" was the reply.

"Well, unofficially, we both know that the Englishman is a soldier with the International Brigade and it shouldn't be too difficult to get them to take him to their HQ in Albacete and there, he should have the best chance of being sent back to England.

But there's something else …

In my house, I have a five-year-old and her father. They are refugees from Baena and I have promised to look after them until they have a way of travelling to Albacete and escaping to England. How can we help the

61

three of them?"

"The car's fixed now boss!" interrupted the mechanic.

"We must talk again!" said the consultant as he drove away. At the weekend, Felipe and Begoña drove up from Jaén.

They heard the latest news. Apparently, as a reprisal for the bombing of Jaén, local authorities executed over 120 Nationalist prisoners. Also, Nationalists had taken several Basque towns and were bombing and strafing small defenceless towns. Then, as a counter measure, to tie down the Nationalist army and alleviate the threat to the Basques, the Republicans had started a major offensive in Brunete, West of Madrid. They all wished it would stop!

After the bad news was out of the way, they had a happy reunion. and the guests would have stayed overnight, but there weren't enough beds for them all.

Birthday Surprise

On Tuesday 11th May 1937, Leo took Rosa to the garage where Manuel worked. At eleven o'clock, Manuel answered the telephone and passed it to Rosa. She had never spoken on the telephone before, but had seen others do it. She looked at the handset suspiciously and put it to her ear.

Her face lit up and she shouted, *"Mama!"* She nodded, *"I'm six … Yes, and I miss Papa too and Grandma and Grandad and Pepe. Don't cry … I love you too … yes please ... Papa! Are you coming to see me? Then is Uncle Leo going to bring me home? Oh why? Yes we go for walks and read a story together every day. Yes, but I'm not very good at it! I love you too Papa!"*

"Here, Uncle Leo, Papa wants to speak to you!"

"Hello José ... Yes we're fine ... We're waiting for an opportunity to get a lift directly to Albacete ... Manuel is working on it ... Yes, Rosa's never a problem, are you, poppet?"

She smiled and put her arms round Leo's waist.

"Are you and Carla well? She's even weaker? And the doctor still doesn't know? Look after her! And, how are Mama and Papa?"

(Leo's Mother took the telephone.)

"We miss you too, Mama! Yes, we're safe here. Give my love to Ana ... No ... the bombing was in Jaén, not here."

The telephone went dead. They had either run out of time or there was some form of censorship. They would never know!

*

Leo put down the telephone and looked at Manuel, *"What a wonderful surprise ... You must have set that up with Aunt Begoña?"*

"Yes, on their last visit, Begoña said that today is Rosa's birthday, so I told her to give this number to your mum and arrange for them to call from a public phone booth. It should have eased their worries. I hope it doesn't unsettle Rosa."

Manuel continued, *"One of the consultants here*

wants you to meet a patient, so let me take you to his ward."

Manuel led the way and introduced them to the consultant who took them into his consulting room. A little later; a patient walked in with the aid of a walking stick. He had a bandage round his head and a heavily bandaged hand. Andrew Banks was introduced to Leo and Rosa.

The consultant said, *"I can only give you five minutes for this confidential and irregular meeting."* He then left the room.

Manuel explained that they shared a common wish to escape to England and their immediate goal should be Albacete.

He told Andrew that the consultant was trying to make contact with the International Brigade in Andujar in the hope that they could agree to a hospital transfer from Úbeda to Albacete for Andrew, as one of their soldiers. He would say that the soldier has a hand injury and also needs a specialist eye operation but wants to travel with the male nurse and daughter who are looking after him.

Unfortunately, the Hospital de Santiago would not authorise the use of one of their ambulances for that distance and Manuel didn't have anything to bargain with to induce the Brigade to provide the transport.

However, he wanted Leo and Andrew to know that he was working on it with the consultant's help and, while they were waiting, Leo and Rosa should come and visit Andrew in hospital. Leo needed to learn how to be accepted as Andrew's nurse.

The consultant returned and Manuel persuaded him that Leo and Rosa should start visiting and guidance should be given to Leo so that Andrew could be released in the care of someone capable of looking after him.

That evening, Leo took Rosa to see a film called *Morena Clara*, a comedy starring Imperio Argentina. It was the first time either of them had been to the cinema and they both loved it. Leo was transfixed by the adorable gipsy girl and Rosa was in raptures at the thrill of the film experience and the happy story. Rosa's birthday surprise was a great success!

The Waiting Continues

Nothing more could be done to help Andrew, but the hospital staff were extremely helpful.

Initially, Leo and Rosa visited Andrew twice a week but it wasn't long before they visited more often, and Rosa became Andrew's eyes, leading him eagerly, hand in hand, as they explored the hospital and its vicinity.

Meanwhile, Leo worked voluntarily as a ward assistant. The nurses appreciated his help and taught him some of the rudiments of nursing. He was soon accepted as an unpaid trainee nurse. The trio had become part of the hospital's daily life. Summer came and autumn followed, but still no opportunity to travel to Albacete.

And still they waited, while disturbing news reached them of the war in the north.

In June, the Nationalists took Bilbao: 200,000 fled

from the city: many drowned attempting to escape by boat. In July, there was a massive Republican offensive at Brunette, with terrible losses on both sides … August saw a new Republican offensive near Zaragoza; Santander fell to the Nationalists who took 60,000 prisoners; Andrew's British No. 1 Company of the International Brigade failed to take Lopera, (where Andrew was injured the previous December).

*

In early September 1937, a small convoy of military ambulances arrived at Úbeda hospital. The commanding officer asked for help from a surgeon and the use of the hospital's operating theatre.

Tom, one of the drivers, drove his truck into the hospital garage and told Manuel that it was unlikely his truck would make it to Albacete … could he help! Manuel could hear that the engine was about to give up the ghost and decided that here was the opportunity he had been waiting for.

He told the driver that he needed to check something first, but felt he could fix it. He immediately found Leo and Andrew and told them to be ready to go to Albacete!

Manuel then managed to speak to his friendly consultant and explained that he could repair the engine of the ambulance by the following afternoon, but only if Leo, Rosa and Andrew could be taken to Albacete with the other military patients.

Confidently, Manuel returned to the garage and soon received confirmation that space would be made in the repaired ambulance which should follow the others once the repairs were completed to the driver's satisfaction. The main convoy would leave the following morning after three soldiers had received urgent surgery and were allowed to recover overnight.

Leo and Rosa spent their last night with Manuel and Carmen, feasting and enjoying each other's company. Rosa didn't read her bedtime story with Leo until after midnight, but then, the others went to bed too.

In the morning, Manuel said he would let Leo and Rosa's family know that they were on their way to Albacete. Carmen gave Leo a large bag of food for the journey and tried to hide her tears as she waved them goodbye.

In the garage, Manuel took out the truck engine, stripped it down and replaced or repaired various parts. The engine was still to be remounted when Tom announced that the patients from his vehicle had been transferred to the other ambulances and the convoy had already left.

Manuel and Tom agreed that it would be best if he didn't leave until early the next morning. That afternoon the work on the ambulance was finished and tested to the satisfaction of Manuel and Tom.

Some of the nurses had heard of the imminent departure of the trio and surprised them with a late-night party and an unforgettable night, not only for Leo and Andy but also for Tom.

Rosa didn't object to one of the older nurses reading her bedtime story with her.

8. CASTILLA LA MANCHA

On to Albacete, (in Castilla La Mancha) …

After the late night for Leo, Andy and Tom, the ambulance left for Albacete, but not as early as planned!

Andrew was wearing his uniform and therefore it was agreed he should ride in the cab with the driver.

Rosa seemed happy to be in the back with Leo. The rear of the ambulance had no divider separating it from the cab. She had more space to move about and occasionally she would curl up on a bunk and sleep for a while, but most of the time, she would sit in the middle, behind the front seats, looking ahead, as the mountainous road unfurled itself before them.

The ambulance was never built for speed and had to be coaxed up some of the ascents and held in a low gear for long steep gradients. They rested themselves and the ambulance at Villanueva Del Arzobispo and Reólid.

On the southern outskirts of Albacete, they met a road block, guarded by an intimidating bunch of armed scruffy-looking soldiers.

Two of the soldiers came to each side of the cab and one of them spoke rapidly in Spanish to Tom who didn't understand what he wanted.

Andrew replied in Spanish and was told to shut up ... They were speaking to the driver! Andrew interrupted and told them the driver was English and they were part of the International Brigade from Lopera, heading for the military hospital in Albacete.

He was told to open up the back for inspection. *"What are these two doing in a military ambulance?"* they demanded gruffly.

"He is a civilian nurse and that is his daughter. He and his daughter have papers from the brigade."

"Why is there only one vehicle? You should be in a

convoy!" shouted the leader.

Andrew shouted back, *"The engine gave up and had to be repaired in Úbeda. We are a day behind the convoy."*

The soldiers moved the barricade and grudgingly waved them through.

A couple of minutes later, Tom said, *"I think the Republican air base at Los Llanos is over on the right there. That would be why we were stopped!"* They drove on anxiously towards the city. On arrival at the hospital, they reported to reception and the duty officer was called.

When he finally appeared, Tom explained that the engine of the ambulance had to be repaired and consequently they were one day behind the convoy from Lopera.

The officer said, *"The others have prepared for going to Cuenca first thing tomorrow. We suffered heavy losses west of Madrid. Survivors made it south of Madrid to our base at Cinchón. Some of the injured were taken to Cuenca hospital but many went by train to Valencia. We are sending a convoy by road to transfer those we can from Cuenca to the Brigade's new hospital facility at Benicasim, north of Castellón de la Plana.*

"The corporal, here, will take you to transport HQ where you will report to the officer in charge of the convoy. You will collect equipment and fuel for the journey. As for the so-called nurse and the child. It's highly irregular but I haven't time to mess about. The four of you can sleep in the ambulance tonight."

As he turned around and briskly marched away, the corporal led them back to the ambulance, climbed into the cab beside Tom, told the others to get in the back and he directed Tom to the Nearby Transport HQ.

The Captain in charge of the convoy greeted Tom with a brusque, *"Ah, you're here at last. Has the engine been repaired and it's serviceable again?"*

"Yessir!" replied Tom.

The Captain gave Tom instructions about preparing for the journey. He looked again at Andrew. *"Let's hope Benicasim can help you, soldier, but I hope I don't regret taking on your so-called trainee nurse and the child. This won't be a picnic."*

"You two soldiers will sleep in the hostal over there, but it's no place for a child. The civilians should stay in the ambulance."

While preparing the ambulance, they found the canteen and checked out the hostal. Leo managed to persuade one of the hospital nurses to let Rosa and him spend the night in a storeroom next to a washroom.

Andrew woke Leo and Rosa at six o'clock in the morning, saying he would meet them in the canteen in ten minutes time. All eyes were on Rosa when she entered the canteen, spotting Andrew, and giving him an enthusiastic shout and a big wave. Andrew could only see her hazily through his good eye, but was treated to a big hug before he could stand up.

After the three had eaten breakfast, they met Tom at the ambulance. As agreed, they left at precisely 7.00am. A jeep with a machine gun mounted on it, led 10 trucks, mostly ambulances. The officer brought up the rear in his jeep.

Rosa took up her usual position behind the two front seats, but after they turned onto another road at Roda, she became bored and Leo had difficulty in keeping her occupied. He was relieved when she curled up on a bedroll and fell asleep for about an hour.

They had a couple of brief stops outside villages, but otherwise, the convoy made its way slowly, further into the mountains and as they neared Cuenca, the altitude was sometimes about 1,000 metres.

At last, they reached Cuenca hospital.

The vehicles were parked in a yard adjacent to the

hospital and a guard routine was established. The Captain announced their arrival to the hospital administrator.

Rosa voiced the thoughts of the convoy's personnel. *"I'm hungry. Can we eat?"*

The four went inside their ambulance and Leo passed round some food he had scrounged at Albacete. *"This will have to do for now!"*

Half an hour later, they were told that the hospital canteen would feed them in two sittings, the first starting in 45 minutes and the second 30 minutes after that.

They were also told there were no spare beds in the hospital and they would all have to spend the night in their trucks. Further general instructions followed.

After dinner, Leo, Rosa and Andrew made themselves reasonably comfortable in the truck, but wrapped themselves up in army blankets to keep out the falling temperature.

Andrew picked up Rosa's book and said the three of them were going to play a new game using her book … She would read a page in Spanish and Andrew would ask her and Leo questions in Spanish, then help each one to answer in English. This established a common interest and a fun way to learn English, but it was never called 'learning'. In the not too distant future, some of the questions would also be in English!

In the morning, when Leo wakened Rosa, he was rewarded with a *"Good morning Papa,"* (in English), a coy smile, sparkling eyes and a big hug.

Andrew pulled a face and said, *"What about me?"*

and "Uncle Andy" was given a similar affectionate greeting. *"You mean, 'Good morning Uncle Andy!'"* he whispered softly.

Rosa looked at the sky, gave him a big smile and repeated, *"Good morning Uncle Andy!"*

*

During the morning, the vehicles were refuelled and prepared for the road once more. The officer and NCOs identified which patients would come and any special needs they may have. After lunch, each driver was introduced to the patients who had been allocated to him and told to make the necessary arrangements for making the patients comfortable in their vehicle the following morning and to be ready to leave promptly at 8.00am.

Tom's team spent the rest of the afternoon with their new patients and the nurses who currently looked after them. Rosa helped them to perk up and asked each of them for their names. With each patient, she learned a few more English words, but wasn't too happy about being called Rosie.

After their evening meal, Rosa drew a picture for each patient and, with Andy's help; she added the patient's name and fixed the appropriate picture by each place in the ambulance.

Next morning, Rosa played hostess and showed each patient to their place in the ambulance. They were delighted when she showed them their own special picture.

Everything went smoothly and, as ordered, the convoy left at 8.00am ... They were on their way to

Benicasim on the coast!

From Cuenca, the journey began in the mountains and the trucks grumbled on, making hard work for the drivers and although it was only September, the daytime warmth took its time to clear away the cool misty air.

They drove south to Almodóvar del Pinar and on to Motilla del Palancar, where they stopped for a half-hour break, before continuing on their mountainous route.

Not long afterwards, on yet another downward slope, Leo shouted to Andy that the truck behind was getting very close and Tom said, *"I've seen him, he's having a problem with his brakes!"*

Suddenly it hit the back of their truck and made it

jump forward and lurch to one side. *"Next time,"* Tom shouted, *"I'm going to brake."* There was another bump, but they didn't lurch to one side. The two vehicles now seemed tenuously linked, and somehow, managed to avoid jack-knifing while negotiating one bend, then another and another. After what felt like a nerve-racking eternity, they reached a straight stretch. Tom braked with increasing force and changed down gears until both vehicles eventually stopped, one against the other.

The two drivers jumped down from their cabs.

"Thanks mate!" shouted the other driver as he nodded towards the drop by the roadside. *"I thought we were gonna take a dive down there!"*

"So did I," agreed Tom, looking at the drop, then closed his eyes and shook his head slowly and repeated, *"So did I!"*

The Captain came up in his jeep from the back of the convoy, *"What the hell's going on?"* The truck driver replied, *"My brakes failed!"* and pointed to Tom, *"Thanks to him, we're still alive!"*

"Well done!" said the Captain to nobody in particular. *"Stabilise this vehicle, drive the front truck forward a little and check for damage before continuing … I'll get the mechanics to drive up and sort you out.*

"The rest of the convoy will move on to our agreed stop at Requena. We will wait there until 1500 hours at the latest, when we will continue as scheduled, albeit delayed."

He confirmed with the mechanics that he had allowed sufficient time for the repairs before instructing the convoy to proceed, leaving the mechanics with their truck to repair the brakes on the other vehicle.

As they drove off with the rest of the convoy, Leo saw that Tom was sweating and his hands moved restlessly on the steering wheel, *"Tom, do you want me to drive for a little while?"*

"No, I'm OK thanks, but I can still feel my heart pounding ... God! That was close!" Leo looked round to see Andy and Rosa comforting the patients in the back.

9. VALENCIAN PROVINCE

By lunchtime, the main convoy reached Requena, the home of some of Spain's best red wine which was probably being produced while they were actually in that area. Unfortunately, they didn't have the opportunity to sample any.

After lunch, their departure was delayed for about forty minutes, to allow additional time for the other two vehicles to catch up. Luckily, they arrived just as the main convoy was making ready to move out … Repairs had been completed successfully. There was almost another hour's gruelling drive before the convoy finally left the mountains at Buñol.

Subsequently, after bypassing Valencia, and stopping to the north at Sagunto, there were sighs of relief when they were told Benicasim hospital was only about forty miles away.

The final stretch was uneventful and they drove up to the hospital just over an hour later than their originally scheduled arrival time. They were exhausted and relieved. It took a further hour and a half for the patients to be settled in to their new accommodation and the convoy crews to enjoy a long-awaited meal and relaxation.

Benicasim Hospital

Back in 1930, a bathhouse and café restaurant was built on Las Villas beach, just north of Benicasim. Three years later, two floors were added to create a hotel with a terrace overlooking the Mediterranean. It was abandoned at the beginning of the civil war, but, because it also had excellent communication links, the military commandeered it and in May 1937 it was converted into a hospital primarily for wounded soldiers of the International Brigade.

It was now September 1937, only four months after the hospital conversion was completed. It was like a holiday resort by the sea. Rosie was entranced … she had never seen the sea before. It was enormous; she couldn't see the other side!

"Look at all that sand," she said.

However, the journey had taken its toll on Andy …

He had intense headaches again, vision in his left eye was limited to shadowy blurs, sight in his right eye was zero and his balance was unpredictable … he relied on his walking stick to keep from falling. Rosa, thankfully, had seen his increased difficulties and kept watchfully by his side, steering him in the right direction and steadying him when needed.

Leo made sure that Andy was admitted officially with the other patients and managed to secure a room for Rosa and himself in the staff quarters.

He was again accepted as a trainee nurse and given medical training, in both English and Spanish.

Rosa was enrolled in a small school which had links to the hospital. She resisted, at first, but soon enjoyed the friendship of other children. Lessons were mainly in Spanish, but English was introduced as a subject in some of the games and songs they sang.

Whenever she could, Rosa would visit Andy and play games or chat to him in English and Spanish.

She would also visit other patients, lifting their spirits by taking them by the hand for little walks and giving them hope for the future, when they would see their own children in England.

Andy was examined and told he would be repatriated to England for medical attention, but it wasn't clear when. In the meantime, he offered to help as a hospital auxiliary where possible.

On 30th October, 1937, the Republican government, which had moved from Madrid to Valencia, moved to Barcelona and the hospital staff worried what it meant for them.

Autumn turned to winter and the cold began to intrude from the mountains in the west, heralding the worst winter in twenty years.

In mid-December, the town of Teruel, at over 3,000 feet in the mountains, was attacked in falling snow by a large Republican division. They laid siege upon the town, but were fiercely resisted by the occupying Nationalists. Two weeks later, Franco sent a large Nationalist relief force which reached the town but had to withdraw to the outskirts in a four-day blizzard with temperatures of -18°C. Fighting came to a halt as guns froze and soldiers suffered from frostbite leading to many amputations.

At Benicasim, Rosa helped to decorate a Christmas tree on Christmas Eve, and then joined in with a group singing Christmas carols. On Christmas Day, Andy and many of the English patients gave Rosa home-made Christmas cards and little presents before having a big meal at lunchtime. Hospital life became more and more demanding with many new emergencies daily.

On the evening of Wednesday 5th January 1938, Leo borrowed a van and took Rosa and two other children into town to take part in the traditional cavalcade of the Three Kings, (Los Reyes Magos). They joined a parade led by the three kings, (Melchor, Gaspar and Baltasar) and threw wrapped sweets to other children and parents lining the streets. The children were then presented to the kings to receive a small present and see a short biblical play.

On 8th January, in Teruel, with no water and little food or medical supplies, the Nationalists surrendered. However, the Republican victory was to be short lived because, with better weather, the Nationalists' advance was relentless, including a massive cavalry charge from the north.

Finally, on 22nd February 1938, with added air support from the German Condor Legion, the Nationalists recaptured Teruel.

There were massive casualties on both sides.

For the hospital at Benicasim, the floodgates had been opened for injured patients to arrive in numbers beyond the capacity of the hospital. Andy helped to look after Rosa so that Leo could give as much time as he could to the overwhelming number of patients. However, the patients also looked forward to Rosa's own special visits to the wards, when, once again, she would bring a smile to their faces and help to make their movements a little easier.

A motorised field hospital had been brought from Teruel and it helped to ease the pressure. However, many were given a minimum of treatment and sent by train to Barcelona.

On 13th March, France reopened its borders for the transit of arms to the Republicans and many of the injured soldiers of the International Brigade managed to travel on the return train journey. The enormous workload had been reduced, but there were rumours that the Nationalists were planning to advance as far as the coast where the hospital was.

Because of this, some staff asked to be transferred with as many patients as possible, to a hospital at La Sabinosa just north of Tarragona. Their request was granted and a group was organised for the journey. Leo, Rosa and Andy were included.

On 1st April, 1938, Rosa was sad to say goodbye to her friends at school. The next day, however, she was delighted to go with a large group of hospital patients and staff to a train station. For her first time ever, she was going on a train journey!

10. CATALUÑA

The train was a motley mix of freight and passenger wagons but that didn't dampen her enthusiasm. Leo was allocated some patients to look after and Rosa grabbed Andy's hand and led him to a passenger carriage.

Once installed, Andy opened the window and Rosa eagerly pointed out and described new things in Spanish. When Andy could get a word in, he would tell her the English words for things and ask her to repeat them.

It took them the rest of the morning to reach their destination, but when the train stopped, some of the Sabinosa staff were already waiting to help them cover the short distance from the station to the hospital buildings.

Firstly, they were taken to a large hall and given lunch. This enabled the hospital staff to introduce themselves and establish the needs not only of patients but the new staff who brought them.

La Sabinosa Hospital ...

The hospital was a massive complex built on a small peninsula between two beaches. It was only nine years old and originally constructed as a sanatorium for tuberculosis sufferers, but never used for that purpose. It was now a military hospital with a capacity of over eight hundred beds.

La Sabinosa Sanatorium (Now derelict)

The picture of the now derelict site shows a central main building surrounded by several separate blocks. It was like a small village adjacent to a railway line. There were streets, tree lined avenues and little squares.

The established staff warmly welcomed their new colleagues who were given assignments within the first 48 hours. Leo was given a nursing role in one of the wards. Rosa was quickly enrolled in a nearby school and travelled on the school bus each school day. English and Spanish folk mixed well and because most of the patients spoke English, language classes were considered as important, especially for the Spanish staff. Andy joined the little group of teachers and he continued to give Rosa special English lessons.

Within the British group of staff there were two or three English radiographers with a new X-ray unit. Leo was attracted to one of them and tried to be in the canteen when she was there. At last, he managed to catch her eye and received a smile in return. She was in her late twenties, not beautiful but very attractive, with a slim agile figure, short curly reddish blonde hair, a freckled face and blue eyes. She had an athletic walk, leaning slightly forward and rhythmically moving her shoulders, which caused her hips to sway. Her name was Jane Morrison.

The nurses on Leo's ward took to him instantly, soon realising that his charming manner and unreserved helpfulness more than compensated for his lack of qualifications and experience. They found out that his birthday was the following week, on 7th April, and planned a surprise party for him at a local bar.

They knew of his friendship with Andy and asked who they should invite. Without hesitation, and with a big grin and a nod of the head, he named Jane Morrison, saying, *"If she hesitates, let me know and we'll work on her together!"*

As it turned out, she had definitely noticed Leo and welcomed the invitation. So Leo had been set up, in the nicest possible way!

Leo knew that some mischief was afoot when Rosa and Andy kept whispering when he wasn't too close.

On the night of his 34th birthday, Leo was told to go to a large van parked in the yard and, when he opened the door, was greeted with boisterous *"Happy Birthday"* shouts and gently pushed inside.

The van sped off to town with Andy and Rosa following in a car. Everybody washed down a variety of tapas with lots of wine, (With the exception, of course, of Rosa and the two drivers).

Jane quickly overcame her initial embarrassment at the obvious matchmaking from the group, but Leo soon won her over and the two clearly enjoyed each other's company more and more as the evening progressed.

When they left the bar, Leo and Jane were ushered into the car and the driver told that the others would follow in the van.

After about five minutes, the driver turned round, *"Would either of you mind if I stop here to go out for a smoke?"* Leo and Jane looked into each other's eyes and mumbled, *"No, we don't mind!"*

The driver stopped the car, got out and walked forward and round a bend in the road.

Leo and Jane exchanged a few words and kissed each other tentatively then passionately and whispered sensitive things to each other. The driver had time to smoke two or three cigarettes before he reappeared whistling noisily!

In the early hours, when Leo entered his little studio apartment, Rosa was in bed, sleeping soundly, and Andy lay dozing on a couch. Leo made it to his own bed without waking them up. He lay there, fully clothed, and fell into a deep contented sleep.

Several times, during the following week, they could hear the Semana Santa drums and music drifting over from Sabinosa village, but few went to investigate.

*

On Good Friday, 15th April, 1938, the Nationalist army reached the Mediterranean at Vinaròs, cutting the Republican zone in two. The hospital at Sabinosa received some of the Republican casualties and there was an increasing fear that resistance against Franco's forces couldn't last much longer.

In the weeks after Leo's birthday, Leo and Jane shared their spare time during the day as much as they could, and Rosa joined them after school. The three of them bonded together happily as though they had always been there for each other.

On 11th May, the school had a lunchtime party to celebrate Rosa's birthday and then in the evening, she blew out seven candles and received new shoes from

Leo, a new dress from Jane and two illustrated story books from Andy.

Just over a month later, on 14th June, Leo managed to borrow a car and took Jane and Rosa into Tarragona for an evening meal in a little restaurant recommended by one of the doctors. Rosa had never been in a restaurant before and, as she tucked into each course, her comments brought smiles from everybody. For desert, the owner and his wife presented Jane with a beautifully decorated little gateau, with a night-light burning in the centre, and led a chorus of 'Happy birthday (in Spanish)'.

"How wonderful," sobbed Jane as blew out the candle and tearfully kissed Leo, Rosa, the restaurant owner and his wife.

*

That evening, the three of them were in Leo's apartment. While discussing what was best for Rosa, to Leo's delight, Jane frequently spoke of, "our Rosa". Leo took Jane's hand and held it tenderly while Rosa watched intently, *"Jane, I love you passionately and I want us to be together forever."*

"Me too," chimed in Rosa. Jane smiled, squeezed Leo's hand and said, "I want that too."

Leo continued, *"We want you to marry us!"*

Rosa followed up with, *"You have to say YES ... say YES!"*

Jane laughed, *"YES!"*

Jane and Leo gave each other a l-o-n-g kiss and all three hugged each other.

"This is my best birthday ever," announced Jane.

"We have found our first taste of peace, deep in this valley of pain," said Leo as he placed a ring on Jane's finger, *"This is **our** birthday present to you."*

*

The following evening, in Leo's room, Andy came in and when Leo and Jane told him of their engagement, he said, *"Congratulations! Yesterday, Leo told me that he and Rosa were taking you out for your birthday and I guessed from his conspiratorial manner that this was what he had in mind ... I wish you every happiness and know that you will be loving parents to Rosa."*

Because there weren't many patients at the hospital, one of Jane's colleagues took a two-week holiday in England. In mid-July, she returned to hear gossip that a major Republican offensive was about to begin and it would be spearheaded by the International Brigade.

Indeed, the rumour was true and during the night of 24th July, Republican forces crossed the river Ebro west of Tarragona and surprised the Nationalists holding the area. However, a secondary attack further south at the delta of the river Ebro was repelled with heavy Republican losses.

The ensuing Battle of the Ebro was to be dominated by Nationalist air superiority from German and Italian squadrons. The Republican and International Brigade soldiers were virtually defenceless against relentless incendiary and machine gun attacks from about 500 aircraft and the enemy's superior numbers of artillery and tanks.

The battle raged on until 16th November. The Republican army and air force was destroyed. Their only comfort, perhaps, was that they had diverted the Nationalists from attacking Valencia. Also, most of Franco's tanks and trucks were lost or unserviceable.

However, it wasn't long before Franco made a new mining agreement with Germany in exchange for more weapons and equipment, which he would use to launch a crippling offensive against Cataluña.

*

In September, Doctor Negrin, head of the Republican government, could see he was staring defeat in the face. Furthermore, since Britain and France had made it clear they wanted to avoid war with Germany, any hope of military aid from either Britain or France could be ruled out.

Therefore, on 21st September 1938, while the International Brigades were suffering massive casualties alongside their Republican allies, Doctor Negrin announced that the International Brigades were to be withdrawn from combat zones.

La Sabinosa, like all other hospitals in Cataluña, was swamped with casualties and severely injured survivors queued in corridors for surgical procedures. Those who could be moved on to Barcelona and possible repatriation or emigration were despatched by train.

*

One day, early in October, Leo was working in his ward when Andy appeared beside him, fully dressed.

"I've been given my marching orders," he

explained.

"Where are you going?" asked Leo.

"They're sending me to Barcelona. I said that you, Rosa and Jane were supposed to accompany me, but they told me that you and Jane couldn't be spared and I was to follow orders!"

"This is my parent's address in England, contact me when you reach England. Give my love to Rosa and Jane."

They exchanged an affectionate hug, wished each other good luck, and then Leo sadly watched Andy go through the ward doors.

When he told Jane, she too was saddened by his departure, but thought it best for him and they shouldn't worry.

Rosa, however, was not so philosophical about Andy leaving her. *"When I come home from school, you and Jane are always working and who's going to read to me and tuck me in at night?"*

Leo didn't know the answer to that, but promised he would sort something out with Jane and the hospital chiefs.

Leo and Jane worked relentlessly. When their shifts finished, they collected Rosa from a child care centre, made it to Leo's little apartment and collapsed silently in each other's arms.

*

At times, Rosa was worried that she would be left forever in the care centre without anybody to look after her.

Late one evening, Rosa's worst fears almost happened when Leo was walking to the care centre to collect her.

Not far from there, near the railway line where it was dark, he heard the muffled quavering voice of a frightened woman, *"No! No don't!"* Then a man's voice, *"Shut up! Hold her still!"*

He took a few paces towards the bushes from where the voices came, but couldn't see anything in the darkness ... then, in the subdued light from nearby buildings, a man's shape emerged, moving quickly towards him. The outline was that of a short slim man, wearing dark clothes.

When he was a few metres away, Leo saw a momentary reflection from a blade as the man moved his right arm. There was no doubt about his intention as the blade was pointed at Leo's waist and the gap closed between them.

In one lightning movement, Leo jumped to the right, across the man's body and away from his attacker's knife, simultaneously drawing his hunting knife from its sheath, and slashing upwards towards his assailant's upper body.

The man screamed as Leo felt his knife strike home. Leo followed up by kicking the man's left leg from under him.

There was a thud and a grunt as his attacker hit the ground. He then tentatively moved to a kneeling position, holding his chest and shouted in Spanish, *"Paco! He cut me, use your knife and kill the bastard!"* Another man appeared from the bushes, paused, looking towards his injured conspirator, then, with knife thrusting forward, took a few crouching paces towards Leo.

Leo, with heart pounding, was only a couple of metres away from the one on the ground.

Facing the second one, he said in a gruff voice, *"Paco! Look what happened to your friend and he had surprise on his side! Come at me with that knife and you'll get worse than he did!"*

Paco took a step towards Leo … stopped … turned towards his friend … then looked hesitantly at Leo.

"Take him to the hospital before he bleeds to death!" commanded Leo, *"Now!"*

With that, Leo backed off a couple of metres or so, glanced quickly at the bushes, but watched apprehensively for the slightest aggressive movement from either man.

The first man staggered to his feet, stumbled and moaned. Paco supported him, as they slowly made their way towards the hospital. They hadn't gone far when they stopped and looked over their shoulders at Leo.

"Get the hell out of here!" shouted Leo, trying to sound gruff and fearless, to conceal his nervous apprehension and anger.

The duo continued towards the hospital building.

Leo went into the bushes and saw a young nurse, kneeling on the ground. With one hand, she was pulling her torn blouse over her breasts, while reaching with the other hand for her skirt. She looked up at Leo, whimpered, and covered her lower body with the skirt.

Leo picked up her white hospital coat which was

nearby. He helped her to her feet and held up the coat, but she clearly didn't want to turn her back on him, so stood facing him, her whole body shaking, while she continued to use both hands to cover her half naked body.

"You're safe now," said Leo softly and gently helped her into the coat. Her bra and pants were somewhere in the darkness.

Holding her torn skirt and white coat across her body, she shuddered violently as Leo gently led her slowly to the Care Centre.

At the doorway, Leo turned round and saw two dark figures following the path to the other hospital building.

Only then, did he put his knife back into its sheath!

The receptionist looked up at them ... *"What happened? You're both bleeding ... You look terrible!"*

Only then, did Leo realise that his assailant had managed to cut his chest, but the numbness was wearing off. Leo asked her to call the Admissions building and reached for the phone. *"This is Leo, Rosa's father ... Two men have attacked a nurse ... One of them has a cut in his chest ... Get Security to hold them!"*

The receptionist grabbed the phone back from Leo. *"Send two wheelchairs here for Leo and the nurse. They have both been injured."*

"I've come for Rosa," announced Leo.

"We'll look after Rosa," interrupted the receptionist. *"First of all, we'll attend to you two!"*

Before the attendants arrived with wheelchairs, the nurse was tenderly ushered into privacy, cleaned up a little and helped into a fresh skirt and blouse. Meanwhile, Leo described what had happened.

Once in the hospital, the nurse was treated and comforted by doctors and friends. Although she had been physically attacked, thankfully, Leo had intervened in time to prevent her from being raped.

Leo received ten stitches to his chest wound, before being bandaged by a nurse who showed even more tenderness than normal.

After the injured assailant had been unsympathetically stitched up, both men were man-handled very roughly by hospital security, then by local police who bundled them into a van and took them away.

That evening, Jane collected Rosa and waited for their hero to join them.

Leo often thought of the promise he had given that he would take Rosa to safety. This situation was becoming less and less safe as the advancing army approached Tarragona. Now he was also worried for Jane's safety!

On 18th October 1938, the radio announced that, yesterday, in Barcelona, there was a farewell parade of over 10,000 volunteers of the International Brigade, presided over by the Republic's president and other leading politicians. It sounded as though those soldiers were already on their way home and Leo feared he was too late to go with them to England.

Family News ...

Leo's feeling of despair deepened as, three weeks later, he heard reports of bombing in the town of Cabra, near his parents' home. He could only hope and pray that his family had not gone to the market that day, as they often did. Communication for the public was limited to radio and politically biased newspapers; long distance private telephone calls were almost impossible.

Some days later, after several attempts, Leo managed to speak on the telephone to Manuel Herrera at the hospital garage in Úbeda. Manuel didn't have any details about the bombing in Cabra and said he would try phoning Leo's uncle Felipe in Jaen and ask him to find out if Leo's family was safe. If he couldn't contact Felipe by telephone, he would drive to Jaen.

Manuel tried unsuccessfully to contact Felipe and kept his promise by driving there. When he arrived, Begoña met him at the gate ... She was dressed in black and ushered Manuel into the living room where the shutters were half-closed, adding to the foreboding atmosphere. They joined Felipe who sat slumped in a chair, forearms on the table, with a cup of coffee between his hands. He looked up silently, acknowledging Manuel.

Begoña made more coffee and said, *"Felipe, you'd better tell him!"*

He spoke slowly; almost reluctantly. *"The seventh of November was Vicente's sixty-first birthday. It was a Monday and Carla and José had arranged to meet their parents in Cabra for the market. Alicia and Teresa wanted to shop for clothes, not only in the market, but also in the shops. Carla wanted to buy some household things and persuaded José to come with her around the market.*

This was all too much for Eduardo and Vicente who selected a friendly bar and sat outside in the shade with a cool drink, while they waited for the others to finish their shopping. They were all looking forward to having lunch in a nearby restaurant".

He continued, *"As you know, Barcelona, Alicante, Jaén and other Republican held cities were bombed by the German and Italian air forces on behalf of Franco. The Republican air force retaliated by bombing Nationalist held Seville, Valladolid and other cities.*

So some Republican idiot, presumably in Los Llanos airbase at Albacete, decided, in his unforgivable stupidity, that Cabra should be targeted as a Nationalist threat! He therefore sent three Russian Tupolev bombers to bomb the hell out of Cabra!"

Felipe drew breath, closed his eyes and picked up the story again, *"Teresa and Alicia were in a small boutique when the first bombs exploded ...*

"The building shook and grey dust filled the shop as bolts of cloth, shelves and racks of dresses fell about them, but the building still stood ... More bombs exploded in the market area. The hellish noise of devastation was deafening. Screaming, banging, crashing as buildings and market stalls fell on unsuspecting civilians outside.

"Teresa and Alicia were dishevelled but unhurt as

they stepped over broken remains of the shop door, into the street outside. They climbed through the rubble amid more bomb blasts. They wanted to get to their husbands!

"On the way to the street where the bar was, they heard whimpering and moaning, screams and shouts from injured and buried victims. Dozens of people were moving debris to rescue those in need, but for some, it was too late. To her horror, Alicia recognised one of Eduardo's shoes. His lifeless leg was sticking out from under some masonry. Two men heaved the structure aside and moved some more rubble to reveal the bodies of both Eduardo and Vicente. Teresa and Alicia wept, touched and kissed their husbands tenderly, talking to them lovingly while they lay peacefully in the dust.

"Carla and José were at the outer edge of the market. Carla was admiring a beautiful bedcover and trying to gain José's attention but José heard the bombers coming in low.

"José saw one pass directly overhead as the first bomb blast hit them.

"They were thrown to the ground but escaped injury. The subsequent bombs exploded a little further away but Carla went into shock and wilted into the bedcover as she dropped it to the ground.

"José kneeled beside her and cradled her in his arms. She smiled, but her eyes were closed. Minutes later, the stallholder spoke comfortingly to José, telling him she said goodbye when she smiled at him!

"José nodded, held her closer and sobbed and sobbed until somebody led him to an assembly hall,

while he desolately carried Carla to lay her beside other casualties.

"He was so distraught, he never thought of their parents ... until he saw their mothers, also grieving over their dearest ones."

Manuel saw how Felipe had almost re-lived the tragedy. *"How can you speak of it in such detail ... so graphically?"* he asked.

"When we heard about the bombing, Begoña and I went to see her sister. We were told about every moment of it, first from Teresa and then from José."

"Talking to Begoña seemed to help them come to terms with it, but both of them are bitter about the war. Firstly, the scourge of the Nationalist advance and now, not the Nationalists, but the Republicans have killed three of their family and, although Leo and Rosa weren't there, they've lost them too."

Manuel asked how they planned to survive.

"Teresa has asked Ana and Miguel to help. Miguel will be responsible for the goats, but Teresa will make the cheese and look after the chickens.

"Ana will work with Teresa to make bread and be responsible for delivering milk, cheese and bread ... Ana will be treated as Teresa's daughter and Miguel as her grandson."

"José will move to his parents' estate to take his father's place. Their foreman will be given José's house and land in exchange for assisting José as unpaid estate manager one day each week. José will buy the grape harvest for blending with the estate wine."

"Thank you," said Manuel, *"I'll do my best to tell Leo what you have told me, but our time on the telephone will be very limited. But now, I have some news from Leo which he would like you to give to Teresa, José and Ana. He has been working as a nurse for the Spanish Medical Aid Committee, caring for International Brigade casualties."*

"It seems that before the end of the year, Leo and Rosa will be going to England with the International Brigade. Also, Leo has met an English nurse called Jane. They intend to be married before going to England. Apparently, the family signed a paper for Leo to adopt Rosa and the couple will adopt her together, so Rosa will have a loving family to support her."

Filipe and Begoña thanked Manuel for the good news about Leo and Rosa and promised to visit Teresa as soon as possible. She and José could do with some good news. Who knows? If Rosa hadn't left with Leo, she could have been killed or maimed in the Cabra bombing!

Manuel had some terrible news for Leo, but after his journey back to Úbeda, he was relieved to be home again with Carmen. After he had been back at work for a few days, Manuel received a call from Leo and he tried to give him the bad news as gently as possible.

"I went to see your aunt and uncle in Jaen ... Your mama, José, his mother and Ana are doing well, but I'm sorry to tell you that your father, your sister and José's father were fatally hit in the bombing.

"Let me continue in case we are cut off ... Ana and Miguel are helping your mama to keep the farm going

and they are doing very well.

"José has gone to live on his parents' estate and given his own place to the estate foreman in exchange for the foreman working as estate manager for one day a week without pay.

"You can be proud of how your family are bravely forging new lives for themselves and how relieved they will be when they hear that you and Jane will take Rosa to safety in England."

For a moment, there was a stunned silence from Leo, before he spoke … *"Thank you for going to see my aunt and uncle … I sensed that something had happened, but this is terrible. It has affected the whole family. Three of them dead!"*

"One day I will have to tell Rosa!" Leo could hardly talk. He managed to say, *"I needed to know. Thanks for finding out … Goodbye, Manuel!"*

"Goodbye Leo … Love to Rosa!"

That evening, Jane wanted to know why Leo was so quiet. After Rosa had gone to bed, she poured a couple of glasses of wine, sat close to Leo, and just kept quiet until he finished telling her his devastating story.

*

By mid-November 1938, the battle of the Ebro was over and more and more casualties poured through the doors, but now most of them were sent on to Barcelona. Hospital workers who lived in nearby Tarragona brought news of bombing raids which could be heard in Sabinosa every day. The school bus stopped going to Tarragona, so Rosa was prevented from going to school … Children of the hospital staff who lived in staff quarters were now looked after in the care centre which had been converted to a dormitory and school.

Soon afterwards, when the priest was doing his rounds, Leo explained that Jane and he wanted to be married. He also showed the priest Rosa's adoption document. The priest said he would talk separately to Jane and made arrangements for them to meet the following day ... with Rosa.

The next day, the priest addressed Leo, Jane and Rosa, *"I see the love you have for each other and how you, Leo and Jane, are committed to each other and to Rosa. If it is your wish, I will arrange for you to be married on Tuesday 22nd November."* They all happily agreed.

*

On their wedding day, Leo waited in the hospital chapel for Jane to appear. He was aware of his rather shabby clothing, but at least it was clean. As he fidgeted from one foot to another, he looked around the simple surroundings and smiled nervously at the guests.

The hospital Commandant and his Adjutant were behind them, acting as key witnesses. There weren't many other guests at the ceremony, but they included the young nurse who Leo had rescued. One of the patients sat at the upright piano, playing soft classical melodies.

Waiting in the corridor outside the chapel, Jane wore a plain apricot coloured dress and white shoes. Over her head was draped a long white lace shawl. She held a small bouquet of roses in one hand and gently squeezed

Rosa's hand with the other.

Rosa wore her new dress of delicate green with white lace trimmings which Jane had given her on her birthday. She too wore a white lace shawl, albeit a small one.

Jane heard the music change to the more dramatic tones of the wedding march. She looked at Rosa, and they both entered slowly and walked up to Leo. Leo offered Jane his hand and Jane accepted it, but had to release Rosa's hand to do so. The couple then saw a hint of dismay on Rosa's face and each offered Rosa a hand, so that she could continue to stand in the middle.

Jane looked at her, then Leo, *"I am so happy we are all here together!"* Leo replied, *"Me too, but I had hoped Andy would be here as our best man. However, it's good he is on his way to hospital in England."*

The priest smiled as he looked at Leo and Jane, then at Rosa, still in the middle, holding hands with both Jane and Leo.

The priest was delighted that Leo asked Rosa to present two rings, (one each for Jane and Leo), and said in a soft conspiratorial voice, *"All three of you are united in marriage."*

After the ceremony, the priest spoke to them. *"As you both requested, with your marriage certificate, you also have an official blessing on the joint adoption of Rosa."*

The Commandant then stepped forward and gave them a stern look. *"It is against regulations for a husband and wife to be working here at the same time."*

He paused, then broke into a broad smile. *"So I have arranged for the three of you to be sent with the next batch of casualties to Barcelona for onward despatch by train to England."*

Leo shook his hand vigorously and Jane threw her arms around him and gave him a kiss on the cheek.

The Commandant blushed, gave a couple of short coughs, and said, *"I haven't finished yet! I have, here, a letter of commendation for each of you for your medical services to this hospital and the outstanding care of its patients. I thank you again and suggest you prepare to leave within the next 48 hours."*

However, because of increased bombing activities of the Condor Legion, they didn't arrive in Barcelona until Monday 28th November, 1938.

Before the long train journey through France, they stopped at Girona and Figueres in Spain. Emotions and fears ran high throughout the journey because some Brigade members had escaped from prison camps, not only in Spain but also in France.

Tales of camp squalor, dysentery and torture were rife and armed guards resolved that nobody from their train would be taken to an internment camp, neither in Spain nor in France.

When the train stopped at the channel port, Rosa saw large ships for the first time. She began a tirade of questions which Leo sometimes had difficulty in answering.

"It's so big and if it's made of metal. Why doesn't it sink?"

Leo thought for a moment and replied, *"If you put a tin can in a bucket of water, it floats."*

105

"And," he added, *"it doesn't stay upright ... But, if you put the right amount of little stones in the bottom of the can, it stays upright and becomes difficult to sink ... It's the same with ships. They have stones in the bottom so it keeps them upright and makes them difficult to sink. It's clever, isn't it?"*

"So how do you know that?" Rosa enquired.

"I read it in an encyclopaedia."

"What's an encyclopaedia?"

"Well, Rosa, it's a special book which helps you find out about things you want to know!"

"Look, Papa, there's smoke coming out of this one's chimney!" and so she happily went on and on!

Rosa was enthralled with the channel crossing and their arrival in the port of Dover.

11. ENGLAND

Finally, on Wednesday evening, 7th December 1938, they arrived by special train at Victoria Station, London.

The euphoria of the survivors was magnified by the thousands of people who welcomed them. Many leading politicians were in the reception group, including Clement Atlee, leader of the Labour Party.

A parade was being organised, with nurses and patients at its head.

Leo, Rosa and Jane were determined to stay together, but looked around for familiar faces of patients and ex-patients in the parade. A familiar voice was shouting, *"Leo ... Rosa!"* and there was Andy ... a few rows behind them.

Rosa ran to him and jumped on him, arms around his neck, nearly knocking him over ... Jane was attending a patient and Leo tapped her on the neck. *"Look who's here!"* She turned around and her face was radiant as she hugged Andy who was clearly delighted that the others had also made it to England.

They joined in the excitement, as the parade went through the streets to be welcomed by flag waving crowds.

After the parade, Andy was sent to Moorfield's Eye Hospital and Leo, Jane and Rosa were taken to the married quarters of a military base on the other side of London, where they were told to await debriefing within 24 hours before contacting friends or family. A female army sergeant introduced herself as their liaison person and helped them to settle into their new temporary surroundings.

There were no problems at their debriefing the following day, especially when they showed their letters of commendation. Leo and Rosa were given British identity papers.

During a break in the briefing, Jane was told that her parents had been informed of her safe return to England and arrangements had been made for them to come and collect her.

The next day Jane's parents came by car to be reunited with Jane.

Everybody was confused by the cloak and dagger secrecy of the authorities who would not be rushed into accepting Jane's new husband and adopted daughter ... They also wanted to see for themselves, how Leo and Rosa would be accepted!

However, Jane's parents were delighted to be told of her romance and marriage to Leo. It was no surprise that they immediately fell in love with their instant granddaughter, Rosa.

Jane's mother, Grace Morrison, looked younger than her 60 years. She had a petite slim figure, a pale face with smooth skin, maybe one or two wrinkles and a few freckles. She wore a flared royal blue skirt and a tailored white jacket over a blue and white striped blouse. Her auburn hair was neatly cut just above the collar of her blouse. Leo thought she looked more like a highly successful businesswoman than the ex-receptionist in her husband's surgery.

Jane's father, Doctor Eric Morrison, eight years older than his wife, was slightly taller and more corpulent than Leo. He wore a dark blue suit, white shirt and striped tie. He had a full head of straight grey hair, bushy eyebrows over steely grey eyes and a soft deep cultured voice. When he peered over his rimless spectacles, it enhanced his professorial manner. He was the senior partner in a small-town medical practice near Norwich.

After completion of some more paperwork for Leo and Rosa, Doctor Morrison bundled them all into his car and headed towards Cambridge. Jane and her mother talked excitedly, hardly giving the others a chance to contribute little more than a brief confirmation of something.

At lunchtime in a restaurant, the intensive talking continued. Finally, they arrived at the family home during the late afternoon.

The house was situated in the outskirts of a village west of Norwich. It was a six-bedroomed house with a large south-facing lounge. French doors led to a well-manicured lawn with a backdrop of rose bushes, lilac, apple and pear trees softening the expansive view of cornfields beyond.

Doctor Morrison also had a study which boasted one wall completely filled with books of all sorts and sizes.

Jane showed Leo and Rosa around the house.

"This is the lounge and these are the family photos ... This one in the centre is of my mother and father, my elder siblings George, (he's 34) and Harry, (32) and me ... and this one shows George, with his wife Marian, (she's 31), and children; Barbara, Simon and David ... Let's see now, Barbara is a year older than Rosa, so she's eight and Simon and David are six and three.

George is a grain farmer and they live south of here, about 45 minutes away by car.

Look on the back of the photo, my mother has written all their birthdays.

Here we have Harry, a Merchant Navy captain, with his wife Sandra and their daughter Laura. Their home is in Plymouth, in the south-west of England."

She pointed to the adjacent room, *"In there is the dining room, with the kitchen beyond ... We'll see those later! This is my father's study."* Rosa looked at the wall of books and asked if they were all story books.

The doctor appeared silently beside them and replied, *"Some are story books, then here we have books about WHO and WHEN, called history books, these are about WHAT and WHERE, called geography books ... This lot answer questions about WHY and HOW ... that's science."*

"OK, Dad," interrupted Jane. *"All in good time!"*

"True!" acknowledged her father.

Jane then led Leo and Rosa upstairs.

"This is my mother and father's room; those three are for the rest of the family or visitors when they come. This one is for Rosa and her cousins Carol and Laura ...

Do you like it Rosa?"

"Oh, YES!" said Rosa, enthusiastically. *"Will this be my bed?"*

"Of course, do you like the pink wallpaper, Rosa?"

"Buenísima!" she grinned, sitting and bouncing happily on the bed while she looked around the room.

They left her there, and Jane took Leo next door into her room … now theirs.

"And this is ours, Leo … I hope you feel at home here … I can tell that Mum and Dad have already taken to you and Rosa … You can both take your time to adjust to England and we can plan for our future in a safe family environment, beyond the terror of the war in Spain".

"Teatime!" shouted Jane's mother from the bottom of the stairs and Rosa came to the bedroom doorway. *"I'm hungry, come on!"*

They sat down in the dining room. The table was laden with cold meats, pork pie, bread, cheese, pâté, pickled onions, and chutney.

On the long sideboard was an array of scones, cakes, and buns which made Rosas eyes light up. *"Look … look!"* she said, pulling Leo's hand towards the sideboard.

Jane's mother sat Rosa down in the chair next to her. *"This is your chair; next to mine … I would like it very much if you would call me Grandma … Now before we have some cakes, shall we try a little of this and this,"* putting a few small things on Rosa's plate.

Everyone smiled, Jane said, *"Help yourself, Leo, this is your home too!"*

Her father began, *"You both have so much to tell us. How you met each other? Where were you married? Leo, Jane told me about Rosa and you taking her away from the war."* They talked animatedly throughout the meal and beyond.

Leo thought about his promise to Carla and José. Rosa had escaped to safety and was already part of a new family!

Indeed Rosa's new Grandma was involving her in plans for Christmas, when the whole family was coming, (although her uncle Harry may still be on board his ship, at sea).

Settling in England

On Friday afternoon, 23rd December 1938, Eric, Jane's father, and Leo went off to buy a Christmas tree. The following morning, it was delivered to the house and Leo helped Eric erect it in the dining room … It was nearly half as tall again as Leo and almost reached the high ceiling in the room.

Jane and Rosa helped Grace, Jane's mother, to decorate the tree and Rosa was delighted when Jane climbed a stepladder and put a silver and white fairy on top of the tree.

Just before darkness fell, an estate car stopped in the driveway and Jane's niece and two nephews … Barbara, Simon, and little David … erupted noisily from its back doors.

Eric and Grace went outside and met the exuberant

attack equally noisily, whilst hugging and kissing their grandchildren.

Meanwhile, Jane's brother, George, and his wife, Marian showed a little more reserve by taking their time to exit from the car and close its doors before calming the children and hugging Eric and Grace.

Grace led them into the house saying, *"I telephoned you with the news about Jane, her husband, Leo, and my surprise granddaughter Rosa."*

George was first to hug Jane, *"Well, my little sister has found a MAN and look, kids, you have a cousin."* He pumped Leo's hand, *"We are the noisy part of the family, pleased to meet you Leo."* Marian and the children gave Jane, Leo and Rosa warm embraces.

Marian took Jane's arm, conspiratorially, leading her to one side, *"I love a good romantic story ... Tell me all about it!"* she said, looking up at Leo's happy face, *"Oh! He is handsome!"*

"Later," said Jane quietly. *"Behave yourself! Firstly, let's settle Rosa and your three little darlings."*

"Oh Jane ... You're a natural mother. But don't worry, they'll look after themselves!"

*

Barbara accepted Rosa as a little sister, although she was only nine months older than Rosa ... but that was enough! Rosa calmly accepted Barbara and her brothers and they soon became close friends.

The boys liked Rosa and thought she was funny when she said things in Spanish ... But Barbara excused them since they were just being silly boys, and couldn't help it!

Grace proudly showed the Christmas tree to her newly arrived grandchildren, then ushered them all upstairs into their rooms. Barbara accepted the addition of another bed for Rosa. She still had her own bed and the little bed for their cousin Laura was there too.

Grace left the children to play in their rooms, but if they wanted to play in the garden, then that too was OK. She would call them later, for the evening meal.

When Grace returned to the lounge, Eric was reviewing the family photographs.

"This one shows George, Marian and the children. Here we have our younger son, Harry with his wife, Sandra and little Laura."

Grace interrupted, *"They've already seen those, Eric. Come and help me in the dining room and kitchen and leave our young ones to get to know one another."* Eric dutifully followed her into the dining room.

Leo looked at the couple. George … an easy-natured stocky, broad-shouldered, man with a bull neck and weather-beaten face topped with an unruly mop of fair hair. George was slightly shorter than Leo and only just taller than Marian, who wasn't little in any department!

She was generously proportioned, with short fair hair, a rounded face and double chin. Her endearing ebullient manner and infectious laugh invited easy conversation. Both were dressed in unpretentious casual country clothes and robust footwear. Their relaxed informality made Leo feel like a well-established member of the family.

At dinner, Eric sat at the head of the table. He had already persuaded Leo to use his bar experience and serve drinks, which he did easily. Meanwhile Grace brought in a large tureen of ham and pea soup. Grace served the children and Marian served the adults. When the soup bowls were empty, Jane took them to the kitchen while Grace took command of the main course. Marian placed a large pork joint in front of Eric who was already sharpening the carving knife on a steel. Jane placed dishes of Cauliflower, carrots and peas on the table then each of them presented their plates to Eric who gave them some freshly carved meat. Marian gave vegetables to the children before cutting up David's meat. The adults helped themselves to vegetables.

The desert was apple crumble and custard, with George unashamedly insisting on his traditional right to scrape out the last of the crumble from the oven dish while Grace shared out the last of the custard among the children.

After the children had excused themselves and the ladies had cleared the table, dishwashing duties were shared among Marian, (washing up), Jane, (drying) and Grace, (putting away).

Meanwhile, Eric poured a glass of port for the men and Leo poured sherry for the ladies.

When the kitchen chores were finished, Marian led the ladies into the lounge where the men were relaxing casually on the comfortable chairs.

"Well, you loafers, where's our Christmas Eve drink?" she demanded cheekily, looking at Eric, as she stood with her hands on her ample hips and a tantalising smile spreading over her glowing cheeks.

"OK, Bossy-boots," replied Eric jovially. *"They're on the sideboard ... Leo has already poured them!"*

The adults talked enthusiastically for the rest of the evening.

As the children went to bed, Grace helped them to hang their individual Christmas stockings on the pegs outside their rooms and showed them the brandy and biscuit on the landing table where Father Christmas would see it when filling their stockings as they slept.

Everyone slept well and only Granddad saw Father Christmas fill the stockings and take his biscuit and brandy!

Morning announced itself loudly at about 7.00am, with Simon shouting to his sister, *"Wake up Babs ... Father Christmas has been."* Barbara appeared, with Rosa close behind, *"Don't call me that. My name is Barbara,"* she said haughtily but quietly.

The children took their stockings back into their rooms to investigate their presents, knowing that they were not supposed to disturb the adults.

Grandma would call them when it was time to open the other presents which were placed under the Christmas tree.

The adults, in dressing gowns, soon arrived in the dining room while the children waited impatiently on the landing, squatting by the bannister, holding the spindles, watching attentively for Grandma to give the signal ...

When Grace called them, Simon led the charge down the stairs, ignoring Grace's call for them to slow down.

In turn, the children read the labels and handed out

presents until the only ones left were for Jane's brother Harry and his family who were expected to arrive before midday.

Breakfast for those who wanted it was informal and more or less help yourself. Slowly, everybody drifted back upstairs to wash and dress for the day. The ladies then returned to the kitchen and set about making the traditional Christmas dinner.

George and Leo were given the job of setting two tables. Two, because they were expecting to seat 13 and Grace felt that it was unlucky to have 13 on one table ... hence, one table for eight adults and another for five children!

It was about 12 o'clock when Jane's brother Harry arrived with his wife, Sandra and daughter, Laura.

Outside the front door, George was standing next to Leo and nudged him as Sandra's long shapely legs emerged from the car, followed by her film-star shape in a figure-hugging dress. With a brief wave, she acknowledged the smile on the two men's faces, then flicked back her long auburn hair, away from her beautiful face.

She then opened the rear door for little two-year-old Laura to jump down and look around. Meanwhile Harry was out and standing by the car, stretching to his full six foot one and twisting his slim body to left and right, with both elbows level with his shoulders. He wore a white shirt with blue cravat and navy-blue trousers.

Harry joined the other men in the lounge, while the ladies busied themselves in the kitchen and dining room.

The girls played quietly in their room, with the boys being snubbed by their sister when they dared to enter the girls' room. The boys then raced around noisily … one minute in their room, another out in the garden, or being sent packing by Marian when they entered the adults' zone.

The Christmas dinner that afternoon was a truly family affair which made Leo and Rosa feel that they had always been part of this family.

The whole family, especially Leo and Rosa, enjoyed the roast turkey, pork, stuffing, roast potatoes and carrots, however Rosa tried one sprout then rejected the others. Grace served the children with Christmas pudding and custard while her Eric poured and lit brandy over another pudding for the adults.

Later that evening, when they all went upstairs, Leo and Jane lay in bed, naked but warm, under the enormous feather quilt which was their Christmas present from Jane's parents. They kissed passionately, and lovingly caressed each other's bodies, feeling contentment without the need or demand for sex.

At breakfast, the following morning …

Harry explained that he had to return to Plymouth with Sandra and Laura because he had to supervise a multitude of preparations to ensure his ship's seaworthiness and readiness for early departure in the New Year.

Marian announced that George had promised to do some of the long-awaited house repairs before finishing some maintenance on his beloved tractor … Later, after a noisy exodus, they left Leo, Rosa, Jane, Grace and Eric to a quiet lunch, contemplating the future.

Rosa would go to school nearby and receive additional lessons in English (She was soon happily established in a local primary school and quickly made friends).

Eric should have retired in 1935, but now, with 1939 on the doorstep, he continued as a doctor at the medical practice, albeit working fewer hours. Eric had promised Leo a position as a nursing assistant at the practice, hoping Leo would obtain a place in a nursing or medical college the following year ...

Leo soon took up the offer and began work at the practice. By Easter, 1939 he had been promised a place in a nursing college in Norwich, commencing September, on the understanding that he would study English and pass an appropriate test.

More of Andy Banks

During Easter, 1939, Rosa asked Leo about Andy, their injured soldier friend, who had journeyed through Spain with them.

Leo made enquiries and was told that Andy had received eye surgery in the eye hospital in London and, for several weeks, had suffered from severe headaches and dizziness. Following that, he was sent to a convalescent home.

The convalescent home told Leo that Andy was given guidance on how to deal with his low vision and received special spectacles, although he also needed a magnifying glass to read printed matter.

He was discharged from the home in February 1939, and went to live with his parents in Peterborough.

The records, did not show that. In fact, after a few days at his parents' home, he needed his independence and moved to a studio apartment in Reading.

Neither did the records show that in December 1938, whilst in the eye hospital, Andy was given a worn piece of paper which he would treasure forever.

It was addressed to:

Andy Banks, Soldado,
London Eye Hospital
Dated: 7th December, 1937
and said in Spanish ...

I am very happy to tell you that on 2nd December, I gave birth to our son, Mateo Andrés and hope that, one day, you will see him and we will all be together Love, Pili.

Leo and Andy should have kept in touch, but because of Andy's depression and Leo's busy life, it just didn't happen!

During March 1939, Andy's emotional mix of joy and sadness, about Pili and his son, developed into an urgent need to return to Spain, via France, before Germany could continue its aggression and possibly invade France.

12. ANDY'S RETURN

On Thursday, 6th April, A few days after Madrid surrendered and the civil war ended, Andy arrived in Paris.

After a week of searching, he found an old International Brigade contact, who introduced him to Marcel Henzel, a Polish antiques dealer, with contacts in the French Basque region.

Marcel predicted that Hitler would soon invade Poland and then France.

He told Andy where to look, in Saint Jean de Luz, (close to the Spanish border), for a fisherman friend, who possibly still made the occasional dubious visit to Spain. He then wrote a brief letter of introduction, (to Kemen Elkano), and handed it to Andy, saying, *"The rest is up to you my friend ... I wish you luck!"*

A week later, Andy arrived in Saint Jean de Luz. As instructed, he went to a small hotel overlooking the port. In the foyer, there was a narrow wooden counter as a reception desk. He tapped the bell a couple of times. A stern looking woman came through a glazed door in the panelled wall beside him. *"Oui monsieur?"*

Hesitantly, Andy replied, in French, *"An old friend of Kemen Elkano told me to ask for him!"*

"And you are?" she added gruffly.

"I am Andrew Banks and Marcel Henzel sent me!"

She hesitated and looked Andy over very carefully. *"He is not here ... Come back at three o'clock!"*

Andy thanked her and left.

When he returned in the afternoon, the same woman answered the bell on the second ding, but this time, spoke in softer tones, *"This way monsieur!"*

Andy followed her through the kitchen, into a cosy but simple living room.

Sitting, with both elbows on a pine table, was a broad-shouldered, weather-beaten man in his fifties. He waved to a chair on the other side of the table and Andy sat down, accepting the offer of a beer. Neither men spoke until the woman had left the room.

After confirming that the man was Kemen Elkano, Andy handed him the note from the antiques dealer in Paris. The fisherman held it in his big hands and read it carefully, *"What do you want from me?"* Andy told him his story; that he had been injured, whilst fighting Franco's army; that Pili had saved his life; that they became lovers; that he had to return to England for hospital treatment and, whilst there, he discovered that he has a son whom he has never seen. And now, he desperately wants to go to Pili and his son, near Córdoba.

Kemen had listened intently and reiterated, *"And what do you want from me?"*

Andy explained that he understood from Marcel that Kemen strongly disapproved of Franco ... That, maybe these days, trading opportunities exist to support voyages to Spain ... Maybe Kemen could find an opportunity to take his boat to Spain. Possibly to Huelva?

"So are you saying that I trade illegally with Spain?" said Kemen, slowly and deliberately, his chin raised defiantly, whilst making eye to eye contact with Andy.

Andy steadily maintained the eye contact and sagely replied, *"I would NEVER speak of such things to anybody but you, however, I plead with you ... Please take me!"*

"I make no promises," replied Kemen. *"You can stay here in the hotel while I make enquiries! Don't talk of this to ANYBODY!"*

In the week that followed, it was clear that Kemen was not only working out a plan, but also checking on Andy's trustworthiness and reliability.

Then, one evening, Kemen put his ideas to Andy.

"YOU are the biggest problem. You're almost blind. You need to become Andalusian and you don't look like somebody from there. Although you speak Spanish well, you have a foreign accent You have no identity papers. You know nothing of life in Franco's Spain ... You have no currency to trade with. You will stand out as a stranger, wherever you go!"

Andy began to interrupt, *"I haven't finished ... I can take you by boat to Vigo, near the Portuguese border ... I know somebody who can then take you on another boat to a port near Huelva, where you will be transferred to a small local boat and taken ashore to a contact who used to be in the Maquis and has been very lucky to survive. (The Maquis are a dangerous group of outlawed resistance fighters, who are hunted ruthlessly by Franco's Special Forces) ... You should not get involved with them. Unfortunately, I have no alternative but to start you off with this contact! Your journey to Córdoba could be very dangerous!"*

"Thank you! It may not be possible to get there, but I am prepared to die trying!" said Andy quietly.

"Maybe you will, but let's see what I can do to help your survival! You need identity papers showing that you are from just beyond the area where you will be travelling. Let's say Úbeda, in Jaén province, where you were in hospital...

"Your parents were from Burgos, which explains your light colouring ... Your accident also affected your memory which comes and goes ... It happened in Jaén when the town was bombed, (You did not fight against Franco).

"Your appearance will make you stand out, so exaggerate it by being almost blind! So don't take those spectacles with you ...

"Oh! As for your accent, learn to mimic the Andaluz accent, but speak as little as possible, and remember, travellers, especially intelligent ones, will be treated with suspicion.

"Finally, how much money do you have?"

Andy hesitated. *"This is everything I have,"* he said, pulling money from various places in his clothing. *"There's an equivalent of about £940 in notes and a few French coins ... My life's savings!"*

Kemen nodded, *"I'm going to need five or six*

hundred of that to cover false papers and something for the fishermen who will take you. What's left, I will change into Pesetas for your journey to Cordoba. You'll also need to change into poor man's scruffy clothes!"

"How much time do you need, before I leave?"

"Two, maybe three weeks, I'll be depending on others!"

One week dragged into another, with Andy helping some of Kemen's fishermen friends by doing odd jobs for them and using the opportunity to learn how he could be useful on the voyage to Huelva. They even took him out for a three-day fishing trip. Naturally, he said nothing of his true plans for the future, although he felt that one of the fishermen did know and was checking him out.

It was July, before Kemen announced that they would be ready to go the next day, on the evening of Friday 7th July 1939.

So it was, they left in darkness and walked to the outskirts of town where they were met by a beaten-up ex-military truck which took them to the Spanish border at Hendaye. Once there, Kemen and Andy were ferried across the river to the Spanish port of Hondarribia, where they boarded a small fishing boat, skippered by Kemen's cousin, Pedro. They slept on board until morning light, when they cast off and began their voyage to Vigo.

While there were no other crew members around, Kemen gave Andy a canvas bag with a cord attached to it. He silently watched Andy open it to find some identity papers, a pouch containing Pesetas in notes and coin, a crucifix and chain, and an old sepia photo of an elderly couple and a small boy.

Andy peered closely at the identity papers in his new name of Pablo Baeza from Úbeda, in Jaén province. He read the details over and over again, then scrutinised the photograph, *(perhaps he could say they were his parents and his brother?)*. He put it inside his dog-eared identity papers and placed them carefully with the money in the pouch.

"Will this be enough money for my journey?"

"That's up to you, my friend!" replied Kemen.

Andy hung the canvas bag and the crucifix over his head, then tucked them into his over-sized stained shirt.

Kemen nodded silently, before adding, *"On your bunk, you also have a bed-roll, a goatskin water bag, a long walking stick and some eating tools. Guard each of these things carefully. They may not seem much, but your life may depend on them! Good luck, Pablo Baeza!"*

Kemen went up on deck and left Pablo, (as Andy now was), to familiarise himself with his worldly possessions and to organise how he would carry them and practice how he would say things with an Andaluz accent.

On the way to Vigo, they fished for hake and in the early hours of Friday morning, they unloaded their catch at Vigo's large fish market, where Pablo was introduced to the skipper of another fishing boat.

The man took something from Kemen, then Andy was told to follow him, having scarcely had enough time to thank Kemen … The boat they boarded, minutes later, was still a fishing boat, but much larger, sadly in need of paint and not exactly the best-looking boat at the quayside.

Pablo was bustled into a grubby cabin and told to stay there until they were well out to sea.

The vibration of the engine announced their departure, but it was at least an hour before the skipper reappeared with a mug of coffee and a hunk of bread. *"It should be a calm trip, so I don't mind you going on deck when you want, but this is a working boat, so keep out of everybody's way, especially when we are hauling in a catch!"*

So, tentatively, Andy explored the boat and found that the galley was the best place for him, partly because the cook was friendly, but also because he welcomed some help, especially in preparing vegetables. At meal times, the crew accepted Andy as Pablo and, although, clearly, they had been instructed not to ask questions, the atmosphere was a relaxed one and they teased their half-blind assistant cook and laughed at his witty responses.

Even the skipper joined in, but Andy was more careful with replies to him.

*

On the afternoon of Monday 15th July, after several days of fishing and carefully avoiding Portuguese waters, the skipper announced that they were approaching the Huelva coast and under cover of darkness, Andy would be transferred to a small boat and taken ashore to the fishing port of Ayamonte.

It was almost one o'clock on the Tuesday morning when, as promised, a small boat appeared out of the darkness and Andy was ferried to a landing place, just up-river from Ayamonte town.

There, he was met by a veiled female figure who took his arm and led him silently to a nearby house. He ducked through the small doorway into a dimly lit kitchen-living-room to be greeted with, "*Hello. Sit down and tell us your story, while Maria gets us a bite to eat and drink! Oh, my name is Juan!*"

Andy gave him his cover story as Pablo, explaining that he was hoping to get help to Córdoba, or if possible, to Andújar.

Juan seemed satisfied with Andy's story and asked his wife, who had been listening, "*Maria, your uncle still takes his fish truck from Huelva to the market in*

Córdoba, doesn't he?"

"Yes," she replied, "He goes on Thursdays, with my cousin Tomas. They would probably welcome an extra hand for loading and unloading the truck! ... Why don't the three of us go and see Uncle Carlo on Sunday and ask him if they can take Pablo?"

Juan agreed.

Andy heaved a big sigh of relief and thanked them both, "I'm longing to see my family ... I miss them so much!"

"OK," said Juan, "it's time for bed."

"Maria, show him his bed! Pablo, will you help me with some maintenance on the boat while you're here?"

"Of course," replied Andy.

Juan smiled, "Good, it's late, so tomorrow, we won't get up until seven o'clock to start work at seven thirty! Good night!"

Andy worked hard at the jobs he was asked to do and Juan clearly appreciated his efforts, consequently, they had become friends by the Sunday, when the trio arrived at Uncle Carlo's house.

*

Maria brought some home-made pastries and helped her aunt to make a large paella. Lunch was accompanied with a generous quantity of wine and Pablo was made very welcome.

In the relaxed atmosphere which followed, the proposal to take Pablo to Córdoba was accepted without hesitation and it was agreed that the approaching holiday month of August should be avoided, so they chose the

Thursday run of 25th July.

Andy looked at Juan, *"If you bring me here again on Wednesday, that will give me Monday and Tuesday to work on your boat! Is that OK with you?"*

Maria interrupted, looking at Andy then Juan, *"That would be appreciated, it will help Juan to prepare for taking the boat out on Wednesday and Thursday, as he had planned ... But don't worry, I can bring you here on Wednesday evening, to be ready for Thursday."*

So that was the agreed plan!

On the Monday and Tuesday, Andy and Juan worked for 13 hours each day, with barely a break for food or drink and, by nine o'clock on Wednesday morning, the boat was ready for sea. Juan was joined by three crew members and Andy said his goodbyes from the quayside as he watched the boat cast off and head for open waters. He walked back to the house for a meal and well-deserved rest.

He had nodded off in an easy chair when Maria said it was time to go. (She wanted to be back before dark).

So, at Uncle Carlo's house, as the old man began kitting out Andy with oilskin overalls for handling the fish, Maria made a tearful exit.

It was a surprise to Andy when Uncle Carlos told him that they would have to be at the fish quay for midnight, ready to load up and be away for 1.00am.

He explained that, to ensure the freshness of the fish, the load shouldn't be out in the sun and they had to be at the fish market in Córdoba by 6.30am.

And so it was, after a hurried coffee and toast, they

arrived at the fish quay a few minutes before midnight, to find Tomas waiting in the truck's driving seat.

The three of them stacked the truck with boxes of fish selected by an agent/buyer. They covered the load with a tarpaulin and tied it down securely, checked everything was to Carlo's satisfaction, then drove away from the port at 12.45am.

On the way, Carlo warned Andy that Franco's special forces were constantly stopping vehicles to search for guns. If they met any defiance or even just had suspicions, the consequences could be brutal and culprits could be sent to the concentration camps.

About six o'clock, after an uneventful journey, they arrived at the fish market in Córdoba.

Once the unloading was finished, Andy asked Uncle Carlos to find out if any of the fish at the market was likely to be collected and taken to Andújar.

"Come with me!" said Carlos and introduced him to one of the sales staff and put Andy's question to him ...

"Yes, talk to Miguel Martinez, over there. Hey, Miguel, someone here for you!"

Uncle Carlos introduced Andy as his friend and co-worker, Pablo, and asked if he could take Andy to Andújar.

Miguel looked him over briefly ... *"Why the bandage over your eye?"* Andy said his friend was killed by a bomb and he was hit by some of the shrapnel. Now, he was blind in that eye and has a wound which was healing.

"If you help me load and unload, you've got a lift!"

Andy beamed a thank you, turned to Uncle Carlos,

"Thanks again!" then looked at Miguel.

"This lot? Just leave it to me!" grinned Andy.

Miguel shrugged his shoulders, not believing his good luck and took a step backwards.

Andy looked over his shoulder at Uncle Carlos and Tomas and shouted, *"Say goodbye and good luck to Maria and Juan!"*

Uncle Carlos kept walking towards the truck, but waved his arm high in acknowledgement.

"They're good friends of yours are they?" asked Miguel.

"Yes, they're a wonderful family," replied Andy, as they climbed into the ancient truck.

*

On the outskirts of Córdoba, a group of armed soldiers waved them into the side of the road.

Miguel warned Andy, *"Be careful, these men are vicious bullies!"* One of them waved a rifle at the cab. *"Get out! Both of you. Papers! Where are you going?"*

Miguel and Andy held out their papers, which were snatched from them. After a brief glance at them, the soldier handed them back without comment. Meanwhile, two other soldiers opened all the boxes of fish and poked around inside before shouting, *"Clear!"*

The first soldier looked at Andy. *"You! Who did that to you?"*

Andy replied. *"During an air raid in Jaén, my friend was killed by a bomb and some of the shrapnel hit me in the head and blinded me in this eye!"*

"Were you a soldier?"

"No!" replied Andy, *"a farmer!"*

"Let me see your papers again!" He grabbed them again from Andy, *"Jaén you say!"*

"Yes!" replied Andy.

The soldier returned Andy's papers. *"Go, the pair of you!"*

Miguel and Andy went back into the cab without delay and drove off.

Andy said to Miguel, *"Does that often happen like that?"*

"Yes!" replied Miguel. *"The bastards are scared of the Maquis!"*

At about 8.30am, they reached Andújar and parked by a market. Miguel asked Andy to help him set up a stall and sell direct from the truck. Andy agreed and soon, a lively trade developed, selling individually to the public and also to bars and restaurants.

They continued until 2.00pm when, although there was still some fish left, Miguel said he was finished there, thanked Andy for his help and explained that he would now tour the villages to try and sell the remainder. Andy took off his fish overalls, put them on the truck, then collected his few possessions and took stock of his new surroundings as Miguel drove off.

He felt hungry, and selected a busy café-bar, but as he made himself comfortable, the waitress came over and said she had seen him on the fish truck. *"Please have a wash before you sit down. You need to get rid of the fishy smell and not put off other customers."*

She led him to a washroom, where he stripped off,

had a thorough wash and changed his shirt (He didn't have a change of trousers, so that was the best he could do!).

When he reappeared, the waitress smiled her approval and told him about the standard meal of the day.

After devouring the main dish, he used some bread to mop up the plate with appreciative enthusiasm. He took his time to finish the meal, then, while chatting a little to the waitress, found out where he could stay for a few nights.

Before going to sleep, that night, his thoughts turned, once more, to Pili and when he had stayed with her. He remembered that she had previously worked as a nurse with her deceased husband in the Andújar doctor's surgery.

The following morning, Friday, 26th July, he made his way to the doctor's surgery and asked at reception if they knew Pilar Rodriguez.

The receptionist was guarded, but clearly knew Pili. She asked why he wanted to know, and Andy hesitated. *"I knew her a few years ago and I want to find her again."*

As he spoke, a door opened, and an elderly lady came out, followed by a middle-aged man who approached the reception desk. He glanced at Andy, wished him good day and handed some papers to the receptionist. She said, *"Doctor, this man is asking for Pilar Rodriguez."*

The doctor looked at Andy more carefully … first, his face, then his hand. *"I remember sending you to*

Úbeda hospital ... Some time ago!"

He looked around at the waiting patients. *"Can you come back at one o'clock?"*

"Of course!" replied Andy, then, with nervous anticipation, went outside to walk about aimlessly until it was time to return.

When he entered the medical centre again, the receptionist directed him to the doctor's consulting room.

After enquiries about what treatment Andy had received for his eyes and a brief look at how his damaged fingers had healed, the doctor asked if Andy was staying permanently this time.

Andy showed the doctor the note he had received from Pili and said, *"YES, I am staying permanently!"*

The doctor saw the emotion in Andy's face. *"I have a house call to make. Would you like to join me?"*

A little later, they were driving slowly through a small village to the south west of Andújar, when the doctor announced. *"The smallholding is just outside the village."* then turned onto a dirt road. *"Here we are!"*

Andy's heart told him that this was Pili's home, although it didn't look familiar.

Then Pili came out of the house. *"Hello Doctor, what brings you here today?"* Andy got out of the car. *"My God, Doctor, its Andy!"*

She rushed round the front of the car and embraced Andy, showering him with kisses. Andy felt her tears joining his and their wet faces radiated happiness.

The doctor excused himself and drove off, leaving

the couple in each other's arms, murmuring words of love, relief, and incredulity.

As they entered the house, Andy asked, *"Where is my son, Mateo Andrés?"*

"He's sleeping at the moment" replied Pili. *"I just call him Mateo, although, as you know, his other name is 'Andrés', the Spanish for 'Andrew'!"*

They were talking animatedly, trying to fill in what seemed like an eternity when Mateo arrived, rubbing the sleep from his eyes.

Pili spoke to him gently, reminding him that his father had been injured in the civil war and had to go to hospital. *"But, at last, he has come home, so say hello!"*

Mateo, with some reservation, gave Andy the customary hugs and kisses and Andy, although thrilled to see him at last, was cautious not to frighten him with over affection, his son wasn't even two years old yet!.

Pili twitched her nose, *"You smell of fish!"*

"You're right!" agreed Andy. *"That's because, to get here, I have had a long secret journey on fishing boats, and then on fish trucks to Andújar..It was an adventure. I will tell you all about it, but I agree, I stink, don't I?"*

All three laughed, but Pili said, *"And we're going to do something about that smell, but first, let us have something to eat, while the water is heating up for your papa's bath."*

It was Friday 26th July, 1939 and at last, Andy was home with his own family!

Fascist Threats

Meanwhile, under Hitler, using conscripted labour, Germany constructed an Autobahn network of over 3,000 kilometres, and had developed the use of so-called guest workers. Efforts were now being diverted towards the construction of the defensive 'Westwall', (the Siegfried Line), opposite the French defensive Maginot Line.

On 1st April, 1939, Franco claimed victory.

Initially, it was assumed that the fatalities would end, but, in fact, there were thousands of reprisals. Also, concentration camps set up in Spain and France. Worse still, many of the prisoners, especially Jews or communists, were sent to some of the notorious death camps in Germany, or conscripted as unpaid, 'guest workers'.

The sabre-rattling between France and Germany continued, and Britain joined in.

Then on 1st September 1939, Germany invaded Poland. Two days later, Britain and France declared war against Germany.

13. AUDIERNE

Corentin spoke to Matias, *"I'm worried for our boys. They may be conscripted into the military. We are probably too old but, there's Josse at 28, Louis at 25, Alan at 24, and Paul at 21. They could all be called up! Will the authorities accept employment in agriculture and fishing as grounds for exemption? Not for long! You did the right thing, leaving Spain, but I don't want to leave Brittany, Do you? What do we do now?"*

Matias shook his head, *"I don't know, my friend ... I don't know!"*

Some days later, they shared their concern with the whole family.

Louis spoke up first, *"I don't want to hide behind fishing ... I'm willing to fight the Nazi bastards!"*

"Language, Louis!" interrupted Matias.

Next, Josse said, *"The Germans have prepared for war ... They practised in Spain!*

"And look what Franco's Fascists did to their own people. My father died in the last war, and Corentin was injured. Our losses will be massive and we could be overrun by them. I don't want to leave Lena and the family to face them!"

Paul and Alan spoke together, *"We are willing to fight, but we're not soldiers. But, if **we** don't, who will?"*

Mavis added, *"I know I speak for Maria and Lena too. The women of our families, hate war. We are proud of our young men, but none of you are soldiers. We don't want to lose any of you to fight Germans or anybody else. Let's not rush into anything! Corentin and Matias will guide us well!"*

Meanwhile, the war in Europe reached France

On 17th September, 1939, Russia joined Germany in the invasion of Poland.

By 6th October, although Poland never surrendered, the country was divided between Germany and Russia. Those Polish troops who could, escaped to neutral Romania.

In April/May 1940, Germany conquered Denmark and Holland in a matter of days, but Norway wasn't conquered until June.

The combined armies of Belgium, Britain, France and Canada were cornered at Dunkirk. By 4th June, over 330,000 allied troops were evacuated to Britain, while abandoning most of their equipment.

France's Premier, Paul Reynaud, and Colonel Charles de Gaulle, proposed to move the government to Quimper and create a Breton Redoubt.

Its terrain would lend itself to anti-tank defence and offered a good chance of obtaining supplies from the RAF and the British and French fleets.

However, General Weygand and Marshal Petain ridiculed the idea, calling Brittany, 'a place of no military value.'

On 10th June, Italy invaded France.

On 11th June, Paris fell to the Germans.

On 17th June, Petain requested Germany's terms for an armistice, then without waiting for a response, all cities, with more than 20,000 inhabitants, were declared, 'open'.

The allies evacuated 57,000 troops from Saint Nazaire and 32,000 from Brest, destroying the port facilities as they left on Tuesday, 18th June.

*

That same Tuesday evening, Corentin and Matias addressed a meeting of the two families.

"Apparently, our Under-Secretary for War, Charles de Gaulle has sent out a radio message from London.

"His message was that this is not the end and has called for all Frenchmen to join him in London and, with the support of the British Empire, with US aid, the Germans will be beaten.

"We do not propose that we all sail to England and join him. BUT, if the younger members of our families stay here, they may be used by the Germans in forced labour camps, as they have done in other countries.

"We therefore plead with you to go to England on the Tanet boat. There, you won't avoid the war, but you will avoid the labour camps.

"We parents will continue here as farming and fishing folk, sharing the Alonso boat.

"You don't have much time to prepare!"

*

The families were shocked by his plea, but after animated discussion, they agreed and began discussing a plan.

The next weekend, de Gaulle's radio message was repeated, and heard on the nearby Île de Sein.

The islanders, (Senans), came to a similar conclusion to the one expressed by Corentin and Matias. So, they made immediate preparations to use several boats, for many of them to sail for England.

Their preparations included collecting supplies from Audierne, where they met Josse and Louis on the same mission.

It was soon agreed that the Tanet boat should join the islanders' boats and sail with them to England.

The two families agreed upon the following plan ...

The Alonso boat would remain in Audierne, skippered jointly by Corentin Tanet and Matias Alonso, assisted by a crew of three volunteers. Mavis would run the farm, assisted by a farmhand.

Maria would run the cottage.

*

The Tanet boat, being the better boat, would go to England, skippered by Josse Tanet, with Lewis Alonso as mate. Its crew would include Paul Tanet and newlyweds, Alan and Lena Alonso.

Monday and Tuesday were hectic loading the Tanet boat with all its fishing gear, plus as many possessions as they could, together with provisions for the voyage.

On Tuesday evening, the Tanets, Corentin, Mavis, and Paul went to the farm for an emotional evening meal, while the Alonsos, Matias, Maria, Alan and Lena stayed at the cottage. For the sake of security, Josse kept watch on the Tanet boat, which he was about to skipper, while Louis guarded the Alonso boat.

Exodus by Sea

Early on Wednesday morning, 15th June 1940, after quiet farewells to their parents, the five left in the Tanet boat for Île de Sein.

Just after the five arrived, the parish priest blessed their boat with three others which were ready to leave. Josse was told that two other boats had also left, two days earlier. In total, 128 young Senans, plus the five from Audierne, sailed from the island, having left proud parents behind!

Falmouth was agreed as the initial destination, although the Senans had previously agreed to go to Southampton and meet the other islanders who had left before them.

The little flotilla left the island in the evening of 18th June 1940, hoping that by crossing the channel in darkness, they could avoid being seen by German warships. They just hoped that they would be safe from the British navy who should acknowledge their French flags.

The weather was unpleasant, with poor visibility in driving rain during the night. Dawn saw little improvement and heavy seas continued to slow their progress.

Late in the afternoon, they were still in open waters, when a British Naval patrol boat approached and scrutinised them closely. After communications by loudspeaker, they were satisfied and offered to escort the little flotilla to the Saint Anthony Head lighthouse at the mouth of the river Fal.

The offer was gratefully received and about an hour later, they saw the lighthouse. The patrol boat told them that the port authority had been informed, and they should wait for a pilot to guide them in. As they were being told of this, a pilot boat arrived. The patrol boat wished them luck, turned around and sped off.

The pilot boat led them to moorings, where they were welcomed by a Falmouth official, who waited for them to secure the boats before taking them to a hall where a group of officials and civil volunteers checked their credentials while they were given hot meals.

The Senans explained that they wanted to continue their voyage to Plymouth or Southampton, because many of them intended to join de Gaulle in London. They were advised to go to Plymouth, where accommodation could be found for those who wished to stay and transport would be arranged for those who wanted to go to London.

The Senans were then taken to temporary accommodation in a church hall, so they could rest, before their onward journey.

The five from Audierne said they wanted to retain their boat and find a suitable port which would accept them in their fishing fleet. Alan and Lena, as a married couple, were collected by a local lady, who took them to her home in Penryn, established them in a cosy bedroom, and made some tea.

Josse, Louis and Paul were taken by an elegant, well-dressed lady, to an imposing large house in Falmouth. A housekeeper ushered them into a spacious attic which had three single beds.

They were then shown around what, in better times, had clearly been the servants' austere quarters, but nevertheless adequate for their immediate needs.

After a night in the church hall, the Senans were keen to reach Plymouth, and set off in the morning at about ten o'clock.

The five had met up in a harbour-side café, to take stock of their situation, so were able to wish their friends bon voyage and good luck for the future.

'The Five' in England

They made enquiries both in Falmouth and Penryn about permanent moorings and rental accommodation. They were soon successful in locating a mooring and concentrated on finding nearby rental property.

The men found an affordable three-bedroomed cottage up a steep cobbled street, close to Penryn harbour. It was just enough for them, without Alan and Lena.

By mid-August 1940, the four men had made their first fishing trip on the Cornish coast and successfully sold their catch. They were accepted as, 'Fellow Celts'!

Alan and Lena's landlady, Alice, had just lost her husband at Dunkirk. They had no children, so Lena and Alice soon became friends, but more like mother and daughter. They would go shopping together and Lena would chat about the farm in Audierne and how she would like Alan and her to find a farm near Penryn.

The four men worked together on the boat. Josse and Paul were happiest when they were fishing. However, the others had lost their enthusiasm for fishing. It had simply become a job to be done.

Alan became more introvert, missing Lena and the farm life they had begun together in Brittany.

Louis was beginning to regret having left his parents to look after themselves under German occupation. He thought of joining de Gaulle and the Free-French forces and in August, Louis left for London … Censored letters became the only contact with him.

Josse, Alan and Paul and Louis had previously agreed to split the boat ownership equally among them, and divide proceeds from fish sales five ways. One part for the boat and the remainder shared equally among the four of them.

A small group of teenagers often hung about by the harbour and two of them, aged about 16, asked if they could join the crew. They accepted the terms offered and the complement of crew was now five.

Towards the end of August, Alice, (the landlady), told Lena that, while making enquiries about tenant farms, she had been referred to the Tenant Farmers' Association. She had then met the local representative and told him about Lena and Alan. Not long afterwards, he called at the house and gave Alice details of a tenant farmer who wanted to leave.

In her little 1936 Austin Seven car, Alice drove to the farm with Lena and Alan. It wasn't far.

The tenant had left his wife to look after the farm on her own, while he went in a friend's boat to rescue soldiers from the beaches at Dunkirk. Unfortunately, the boat was sunk by German fighters and the sole survivor was not her husband. She could no longer manage the farm, and wanted to go and live with her sister in Truro.

It was a sad story, but it gave Lena and Alan the opportunity they wanted.

Two weeks later, Lena and Alan signed a tenancy agreement and moved into the farm. Fortunately, most of the furniture had been left for them, since there was no room for it in the sister's house in Truro. In addition, they also acquired an old tractor with the farm.

Lena and Alan were ecstatic, but, sadly, Alice had lost her house companions. However, they continued to meet, at least once a week.

Josse and Paul were pleased for Alan and Lena, but missed him as a crew member. Josse initially intended to continue with a reduced crew of only four, but Alan proposed that, since he and Louis were no longer crew members, but still part owners of the boat, they should reduce their share of the proceeds by half, on the understanding that another crew member be employed. Josse and Paul agreed, but suggested that Louis's full share be banked separately until they had Louis's agreement to the new arrangement.

In November, Alice brought Lena a letter from Louis, saying that he had joined the Free French forces at a training camp somewhere in England. He was with a great bunch of people and learning a lot.

During the summer and autumn of 1940, the Luftwaffe tried to defeat the RAF, but failed. However, in September, the Germans began heavy night bombing raids, causing a massive death toll and destruction. All the major ports and industrial cities suffered, especially London, but the British spirit was defiant.

Christmas celebrations for 1940 were held at Alan and Lena's farm. Alice helped Lena with the cooking and she was accepted by Lewis and Paul as an 'honorary mother'.

Tender thoughts were expressed about their parents in Brittany and Louis, 'wherever he is'.

In a toast to *'Our Family'*, Alice and the brave husband she lost were especially included.

The War in Brittany

Meanwhile, in Brittany … Brest and Lorient were being used to service German warships and house U-boats, which attacked the convoys ferrying supplies from the US to Britain.

In Brittany, as the Germans developed the strategic importance of the ports of Brest, Lorient and Saint Nazaire, a three-kilometre shoreline zone was established, as part of a defensive 'Atlantic Wall'.

Within this zone, residents were told to leave their homes, without taking their furniture or household items, thus making them available for billeting German forces.

The zone was enforced between Quimper, Concarneau and Lorient, but relaxed in Audierne Bay. However the activities of fishing boats were monitored by the Nazi regime, (including collaborators and sympathizers). In practice, the boats were confined to small flotillas, so one observer could ensure British boats were not transferring people or weapons to the Breton boats. As suppliers of food, those employed in fishing and farming were excused from forced labour camps, provided they were not seen as a threat.

In Audierne, there was a token presence of German soldiers, who reported to their superiors in Quimper.

One Monday, a jeep stopped outside the cottage and an officer and a corporal got out. The officer knocked on the cottage door. Tentatively, Matias silently opened the door and looked at them.

The officer handed him a document and spoke in a slow, accented French…

"This is an order from Quimper, for you to accommodate one of our soldiers from next Monday onwards … That will be Corporal Schultz, here! We will return on Friday to confirm that the arrangements you have made are satisfactory. Have you any questions?"

Matias looked at the paper, written in German, swallowed and looked up … *"No, no questions!"*

"Good!" was the abrupt reply. The officer and the corporal returned to the jeep and drove off.

Matias closed the door and turned to María who had been standing behind him. *"Did you hear that?"*

"Yes," she sighed, *"Thank God Louis is not there to make unacceptable comments."*

*

On Friday, as promised, the jeep returned and María took the two soldiers to Louis's bedroom then showed them around the house.

The officer asked if either of the two vacant bedrooms were normally occupied. María explained that their daughter was now married and had left home, and their son had also left home.

The officer told the corporal that he was a lucky man, to have such accommodation. The corporal agreed.

Before leaving, the officer stood to attention, *"Good, I don't expect any trouble, neither from my corporal, nor from this family! Corporal Schultz will return with his things on Monday."* He opened the door, *"Good day!"* and they left.

On Monday, at 9.00am, Corporal Schultz arrived. He was slightly smaller than Matias, but, at 45, was three years younger. His uniform, strained slightly at the buttons, betraying his tendency to eat more than he exercised. His small hometown of Achern, at the edge of the Black Forrest, and close to the French border, explained his rudimentary knowledge of French.

He didn't spend long in arranging his few possessions and explained that he was to report to the town hall for 10.00am sharp.

María guessed that, if she fed him well, and treated

him like a distant cousin, he shouldn't be too much of a burden. However, careless talk was to be avoided.

At the farm, Corentin and Mavis were rarely visited by Germans, but on their visits into town, they had to be careful, especially if Corporal Schultz's relaxed manner invited them to drop their guard.

Their neighbour's son still worked for them as a farm labourer and that seemed to be accepted by the German administration.

In January, 1941, Louis, and Oskar, a Polish army officer, were being briefed, in French, at the training camp in England.

14. NORFOLK

Britain was now at war with Germany

Eric finally retired on his 70th birthday, in July 1940, but continued to mentor Leo in his studies.

Jane, with Eric's help, was able to find a suitable position in Norwich hospital … (She was given a temporary nursing appointment in Norwich, and was soon given a permanent position as a radiographer).

Leo, Jane and Rosa continued to live with Jane's parents.

As a wartime precaution, many children were evacuated from large industrial cities, especially London and placed with families in the coastal towns of Norfolk and other areas. However, after Dunkirk in June 1940, there was a fear of enemy landings, so evacuees were relocated away from coastal targets such as Cromer and sent to more rural locations.

In addition, more evacuees were arriving from London.

Consequently, in January 1941, the authorities allocated the Cooper family to Eric and Grace's house.

There was Mary, the mother, (aged 26), Anne (aged 5) and Sally (aged 3). Mr Cooper, (Sam), was one of many soldiers who died on the beach at Dunkirk.

Grace drove to Norwich to collect them from the station.

The train had just disgorged its passengers onto the platform. There was an aura of uneasy quietness, despite the number of people, (mostly children). Our little trio, with their coat collars turned up against the fresh wind, looked so sad and lost. Each was clutching a small suitcase and was looking vainly for a friendly face.

Several ladies, lists in hand, were matching evacuees to their sponsors and Grace was soon introduced to the Cooper family, who shuffled obediently behind Grace, as she led them to the car. The two children didn't want to be separated from their mother, so Mary sat in the back with them.

On arrival, Grace showed them around the house.

Rosa's room had two extra beds in it, to allow for visits from the other grandchildren … Mary would use the room which had been reserved for visits from Grace's son Harry and his wife. *(George and Marian were more regular visitors and they would still have their room.)*

Sally held Rupert, her teddy bear, close to her chest and clung to her elder sister, Anne.

Rosa showed them around and the three girls gradually accepted the new situation.

During school term for Rosa and Anne, Grace usually walked them to and from school since the petrol rationing wasn't enough for her to use the car. Meanwhile Mary, in addition to looking after Sally, helped in the kitchen and took over some of the general household duties.

Sadly, in March 1941, they received bad news about Harry, Jane's younger brother. His ship was torpedoed on an Atlantic run and there were no survivors. The news never reached Sandra and Laura, (his wife and daughter), because their house took a direct hit when the blitz targeted the nearby docks … Mercifully, they were killed instantly!

One day, when Grace was sitting in the kitchen, reminiscing tearfully about the loss of Harry and little Laura, Sally climbed onto Grace's lap and put Rupert against Grace's chest …

"Give him a cuddle … He makes your tears go away!"

Grace did as she was asked and whispered, *"But I need to hug you too!"*

Grace closed her eyes to compose herself.

"You're right my darling … How clever! Shall we have one of those biscuits from the tin?"

During the week, when Rosa and Anne came home from school, Sally would join them and, after dinner, the three would spend most of their time together, mainly in their room.

*

As Christmas approached in 1941, Grace was delighted that her son George and his family would come for a few days … Once again, they would have a full house for Christmas!

Grace thought about how to accommodate the

children … George's boys, Simon and David, would again have their old room … George had promised to swap Laura's bed for a bigger one which Anne could share with Sally, her little sister, allowing the four girls to squeeze into Rosa's room, with Rosa and Barbara retaining their usual beds.

Encouraged by publicity from the Ministry of Food, Mary had previously bought some baby chickens which she looked after diligently – and, before long, their eggs were supplementing the meagre rations.

Christmas food was significantly restricted and presents for the children proved challenging … Mary badgered Grace for old dresses and curtains and produced new dresses for all four girls … Leo raided Eric's garage and made a model aeroplane for Simon and a little flatbed truck for David … The children were delighted with their presents, accepting that times were difficult.

For Christmas dinner, a couple of Mary's largest chickens were sacrificed and these were complemented by a mixture of home-grown and bought vegetables. For dessert, Grace produced her special apple pie and custard. Drinks included George's home-made beer and Marian's non-alcoholic cordials.

After dinner, the adults shared two bottles of wine which Eric had kept hidden and, inevitably, they talked about the war. It was hoped that, with Germany attacking Russia in June, the Luftwaffe would reduce its bombing of Britain and divert its attention towards the East.

Also, although, at the beginning of December, the Japanese attack on Pearl Harbour was a shock to the Americans, the family supported the popular British view that, 'at last' the Americans would join the Allied forces, giving hope that the Allies would eventually win.

(The public weren't told, until the New Year, that Hong Kong had surrendered to the advancing Japanese army on Christmas Day.)

During the following wartime years, fear of invasion disappeared, and although German bombing continued, the increased activity from RAF and American air bases in East Anglia gave a real and moral support to the confidence that the Germans would be defeated. The enemy soldiers were not present on mainland Britain, unlike the Spanish Civil War, when advancing Nationalist soldiers had caused a relentless fear in the civilian population. Leo felt that their life in England had proved to be a much safer place and justified the decision to bring Rosa away from Spain.

15. LOUIS AND THE FREE FRENCH

In January, 1941, at the training camp in England, a note was made about Lewis. *'Alonso can set on fire a stubborn passion within himself, to achieve something he has set his Spanish heart on achieving.'*

Subsequently, Louis, and Oskar, (a Polish army officer), were being briefed …

"Alonso … In June last year, the Polish army evacuated many of their troops from Saint-Nazaire. The remainder made a fighting retreat south to Saint-Jean-de-Luz, where most of them, including Oskar here, were able to board ships for Britain. However, a handful of Poles stayed behind to join a resistance group, 'the Maquis'. We want the two of you to join them.

"Louis … You know Saint-Jean-de-Luz. You speak Basque and French and you have experience as a fisherman in these waters. Your job will be to bring in supplies by boat.

"Oskar … You speak Polish and French and have suitable military experience. Your job will be to liaise with Louis and HQ: Also, to train the maquis in sabotage and survival and supply them with available resources.

"I will leave you together and come back in one hour to answer any questions. You have writing material there to make notes!"

The hour passed quickly and Oskar had made notes.

On his return, 'The Colonel' answered almost all of their questions. The remainder were dismissed with, *"Sort that out between you!"* or *"It's in hand!"*

"Here are your new identity papers, which use your existing forenames, except that Oskar is now spelled the French way, with a C instead of the Polish way, with a K.

"Your contacts here, have allocated code-names, with their usual sense of humour ...

"Louis, your codename will be 'Hook'.

"Oskar, you will be 'Line', and HQ will be known as 'Sinker'.

"Remember, as you have been instructed, do not divulge any information, other than that shown on your identity papers. Tomorrow, at 0800 hours, you will be briefed with available details. You then have three days to solve any problems."

At 2100 hours on Tuesday 21st January 1941, two miles north of Saint-Jean-de-Luz, the submarine commander made contact with a trainera, (a sail-fishing boat, about 12 metres long). A small boat was launched and, after three trips, Louis, Oscar and a load of equipment were successfully transferred. The submarine, 'Sinker Two', then submerged without delay.

Still under cover of darkness, a reception party was waiting on a small beach.

Louis and Oscar each carried a backpack. Boxes were put into nets and carried between two members of the group.

They walked inland for some time, checking they had not been seen. After carefully crossing a railway line, and resting every so often, they arrived at an isolated barn.

Two of the group stayed with them, but, with Oscar's prior approval, the others left with most of the boxes. One of their companions opened his backpack and produced some beer, bread and sausage.

They shared out a little of it, but left some for the morning. The remaining hours before dawn were spent on straw bales covered with loose straw.

Surprisingly, they slept well and didn't realise until morning that their companions had taken turns of being on watch. Oscar thanked them, but insisted that they were not tourists … they were part of the same team, and should share watches equally.

After breakfast, they were taken closer to the Rhune Mountain and introduced to one of the Maquis leaders, who was expecting them.

Before leaving England, the new identity papers which 'The Colonel' had given them, established Louis as a fisherman and Oscar as a shepherd. The Maquis leader scrutinised them and confirmed that the papers would establish Louis as a cousin of a local fishing family, whom he would meet shortly.

He then addressed Oscar, *"Unfortunately, my friend, you are not so fortunate. Because of Germans and local sympathisers, (who could be pro-Vichy or Basque nationalists), you cannot stay in one place for long.*

"Where possible, we will shadow each other."

About 10.30 am, Louis was introduced to a wiry wrinkle-faced, middle-aged man, who identified himself as the skipper of a fishing boat and head of the family who were going to 'adopt' him.

He fired a string of questions at Louis, testing his experience as a fisherman and his language ability in Basque and French.

"What have you got against the Germans?" he demanded gruffly.

Louis replied passionately, *"Their atrocities against the Spaniards, the communists and the Jews ... Guernica ... concentration camps ..."*

The skipper held up both hands to stop Louis, *"That'll do for me, lad, I feel the same way!"*

He turned to the Maquis leader, *"Have you checked his papers?"*

"Yes, their good!*"* was the immediate reply.

The skipper inclined his head to Louis, *"Then let's go!"*

After brief farewells, they set off at a brisk pace and were back again at Saint-Jean-de-Luz for lunchtime.

The 'Skipper' introduced himself as, 'Ander Ochoa', his wife, 'Joska' and his 16-year-old son, 'Iñaki'.

All three accepted Louis, cautiously, while they sat down to a spicy lamb stew.

Louis asked about the fishing and what kind of boat they used. Slowly, they realised that he had genuinely fished in the Bay of Biscay and the conversation became more relaxed.

They asked if he intended to stay, or was he just passing through. Louis avoided answering but asked directly,

"Do you know that I want to smuggle in supplies for the Maquis? It could put us all in danger!"

Ander looked at his wife and son and replied, *"Of course we know that! ... Iñaki and I have done one or two trips ourselves, but need help, so we asked the Maquis, and now **you** are here!"*

Louis said, *"I understand that the German soldiers, based in the north of this region, have established a very bad reputation. I hope they haven't caused much trouble here! ... I suggest that, as soon as possible, we should be seen together, fishing ... and you can introduce me around the harbour and point out any known collaborators."*

"Yes, of course!" replied Ander.

Iñaki showed Louis his large attic bedroom. *"That's your bed there!"* he said, pointing to one of two divans, each of which had a colourful duvet on top,

"You can put your things in this chest of drawers, but we'll have to share the hanging space in the cupboard".

"Thanks, that's fine!" replied Louis, as he sat on his bed and looked around … *"Was this someone else's bed? It looks homely!"*

Iñaki recalled … *"Well, in a way … We had a Polish officer living with us for a little while, but he was evacuated, last year, with thousands of other Polish soldiers and civilians. We used every available boat to ferry them out to ships anchored offshore."*

"So I've heard, Iñaki. The sea was rough, wasn't it? It must have been difficult, transferring them onto ships?"

"Yes, most of them had to leave their possessions behind. The Maquis collected up weapons and ammunition and even a couple of motorbikes.

"We didn't want the Germans to have anything, so we distributed some things among the villagers, cached a lot, and burned the rest."

The next day, after a well-earned sleep and a wholesome breakfast, Anders and Iñaki introduced Louis to the rest of the boat's crew and they joined several other boats on a joint two-day fishing trip.

For Louis, when he was at sea, it was like the life he had known before he and his family had left for Brittany. Once again, he was part of a crew, each one looking after the other. However, back on land, every movement, every word, every contact was controlled to avoid unwanted interference from the Germans. Whenever a truckload of soldiers arrived, the tension was palpable. However, so far, the Germans seemed to be more interested in Bayonne than in Saint Jean.

One day in February, Ander told Louis that they should meet Oscar in a bar by the beach. Oscar told them that some supplies were to be transferred to their boat during their next fishing trip.

"In Spanish waters, a British vessel will transfer a fishing net to a Spanish boat, identical to one in our flotilla. The board, bearing the boat's name, will be changed to be the same as its sister in our flotilla.

"In the net there will be fish boxes containing special items, but the net will remain in the water.

"While the identical boats are in open waters, the one from our fleet will drift away from the fishing flotilla and meet its sister.

"The crews of each boat will change over. Then, the substitute boat will join the flotilla and the crew will make themselves be recognised.

"It will then come alongside our boat, asking for our mechanic to help repair an engine fault. Meanwhile, the net will be surreptitiously attached to our boat before our mechanic returns to our boat.

"The substitute boat will then drift away from the flotilla, exchange crews again, and the original boat will return to the flotilla. You will then bring the second net on board, and put the boxes with the rest of our 'catch'.

"The reason for this subterfuge is that we know a

German collaborator regularly sails in your flotilla, to watch for illegal activities. This way, his suspicions should not be aroused, because he will only see the normal boats and the familiar crews. When you return to port, men from the fish warehouse will identify themselves with the codename 'marmitako' and collect all your catch, including the special boxes."

Oscar summarised what he had just said, confirmed it was understood, and that they would do exactly what was asked of them.

"For security reasons, you will not know in advance, which other boat is involved until its skipper asks for help repairing his engine."

The following week, the usual flotilla left harbour. Their fishing trips could last for up to three days. This time, since the agreed fishing zone was some distance from Saint Jean de Luz, it was to be a three-day trip ...

On the first day, the flotilla kept together, heading for the agreed zone.

On the second day, the boats were further apart, in search of fish. Lewis kept speculating about the movements of each of the other boats.

First one would separate from the flotilla, then another, but everything seemed to continue as normal.

They lost sight of two boats ... On Ander's boat, they continued to fish, but it was difficult for Lewis to avert his gaze from where the other boats were last seen. The two boats reappeared and came closer to the pack, but neither approached Ander's boat.

Dusk was approaching, when one of the two boats

came closer and the skipper hailed them …

"We are having a problem with our engine, could your mechanic please help us?"

Ander agreed, and the mechanic went in a dinghy to give assistance. Meanwhile, a net was transferred to Ander's boat, while onlookers were watching the dinghy.

The mechanic returned in the dinghy. The other boat moved away, after their skipper thanked Ander.

Before hauling the additional net on board, Ander briefed the crew, simply telling them that this catch was to be put with their own, and nobody must ever know about the extra boxes.

On the third day, the flotilla regrouped as the sun rose and headed back to port.

As they moored up, a gang leader from the warehouse spoke to Ander, *"Tonight, I'm having a marmitako fish stew with the family … It's my favourite!"*

The complete catch was loaded onto a truck, which left for the warehouse.

Ander quietly addressed the crew, *"Remember, no gossip! We helped to save the other boat's catch … So, what's a few extra fish!"*

Ander soon returned the other boat's net.

While shopping, Ander's wife, Joska, was asked by a friend if she would act as a guide for escapees heading for Spain. She asked for more information and explained that she would have to discuss it with her husband.

A few days later, Joska took Ander to meet the friend. They said they were willing to help, but would prefer if their cousin, Louis, would do it. Back at home, they discussed it with Louis and he agreed to help, when he was not at sea.

Shortly afterwards, Louis was contacted and, early the following day, he went to a house near the town hall, where he met a thick set man who had done several runs as a guide for escapees to Spain. *"Today, we will meet someone and take him to the Spanish border. He is an English airman who was shot down. You will come with us, to learn the route and meet the contact. Come ... We will collect him."*

They took the bridge over La Nivelle river and skirted around Cibure, to the cemetery, where a man was kneeling by a grave. Louis's companion spoke to him in French, *"It's cold here, I know a warmer place, shall we go there?"*

The man looked up and smiled, *"Oui monsieur!"*

The three then headed for Olhette, to the south.

The airman confirmed that he was a bomber pilot and, ten days earlier, had been shot down over Brittany. The rest of his crew had been captured by the Germans.

After about an hour, they stopped in a secluded area and Louis's companion produced a flask of coffee and a baguette, most of which was given to the pilot.

They trekked on for about another two hours on ancient routes until they reached the outskirts of Olhette, where they cautiously approached a farmhouse. Louis's companion recognised a sign that it was safe and they knocked on the door.

They were welcomed, and rested their legs, while enjoying a hot meal and drinking some local wine.

However, they couldn't afford to stay for long, so thanked their hosts and, once more, headed south on the chemin de Inzola.

As they approached the Spanish border, they could see the Ibardin peak ahead, to their right, and continued on back-roads until they reached a ruined farm building. They checked it out carefully, but there was no sign of life, so Louis's companion slowly walked up to the front of the building, looked around the back and inside, then waved the others to join him.

After about fifteen minutes, a figure emerged from the trees and slowly walked up to them. He quietly spoke an agreed password and Louis's companion responded accordingly. A few pleasantries were exchanged. The pilot was unceremoniously passed on to his next guide and the two disappeared into the trees.

Louis's companion said, *"That's it!"* and the pair started their return journey.

On the way, his companion explained to Lewis that they had probably passed on the pilot to one of the legendary border smugglers, the 'mugalari', who for centuries have evaded French and Spanish authorities, smuggling contraband. Now, their hatred of fascists was being used to the advantage of those needing to escape the Nazi occupation.

When Louis returned to his new home, Ander and Joska were relieved to see him, but merely asked if all went well. Louis assured them that there were no problems.

In the months that followed, Louis made other trips to

the border, but one of them was alarming!

Louis was guiding two escapees on the route to Olhette. Fortunately, they kept off the road when they could, but an old Citroën van came up on the road behind them. It stopped and asked one of the escapees for directions.

The escapee shrugged his shoulders in a very Gallic fashion and turned to Louis, *"Philippe?"*

Louis quickly responded in verbose Basque and the driver mumbled, *"Why can't these damned folk speak French?"* and drove off. The three heaved sighs of relief, but Louis warned them that the driver was no local and could have been a collaborator. He did, however, compliment the escapee's quick thinking in calling him 'Philippe', not panicking and not stumbling with his limited French.

*

Early in the spring of 1943, Oscar informed Louis that the Gestapo had caught a group of resistance fighters, escape organisers and escapees South of Bayonne. They took a few for interrogation and shot the rest, who were left where they were murdered. The local people buried them and warned others to be more careful.

One evening, in May, Oscar came to the house and explained to Louis that a British officer, who had urgent secret information, would be arriving at the cemetery pickup point. He was to be taken by Ander's boat to another fishing boat, from Hondarribia. That boat was to transfer him to a submarine in open waters. The timing wasn't yet certain, but it would be short notice.

Two days later, Oscar collected Louis at night, and took him to a meeting place near the cemetery. In darkness, they met two other men and as they were about to move away, shots rang out. Oscar was killed instantly.

One of the others was hit in the chest. He produced a waxed cloth envelope from inside his jacket and handed it to Louis.

"This must reach England urgently."

Louis took the blood-stained envelope.

There was another exchange of gunfire, then silence.

All three of Louis's companions were dead and Louis couldn't see their assailants!

Louis crouched and ran in a direction which he hoped was to safety. He stopped and listened for any pursuit, but the only noises came from nearby houses, where residents had been disturbed.

Cautiously, Louis made his way home.

Ander and Joska, were waiting up for him, expecting him to bring a British stranger. Louis was shaking.

"What's wrong?" asked Joska.

"Oscar, the British escapee and his companion were all killed!" replied Louis, almost sobbing.

"Ander ... Tomorrow, you have to take me in your boat and transfer me to another boat, so I can take this envelope to England."

Ander replied, *"That's OK, I knew the plan was to take the Englishman, but, sadly, that now means you will be leaving us!"*

"Yes, it does! You have all made me feel part of your family and I will miss the comfort you have given me."

They were all up early, as usual, preparing for another fishing trip. After breakfast, Joska filled Louis's rucksack with food and wine, for his journey to England.

Before following Ander and Iñaki to the boat, Louis kissed Joska twice on each cheek, while giving her a long embrace.

The flotilla assembled, (including the watchful collaborator), and left port.

They were following arrangements set up with Oscar and, as planned, Ander's boat kept with the fleet on the first day. It was not until the second morning, while there was still a haze, that Ander's boat moved away from the fleet. The sea was calm, so the other boat came alongside and Louis jumped across and said goodbye to Ander and his crew.

Ander's boat disappeared quickly and rejoined the flotilla.

The skipper of the other boat was unaware that his passenger had been changed and, since it made no difference, Louis didn't tell him.

"The submarine should meet us in forty minutes."

"That's good," said Louis, as he looked around the boat, which looked very similar to the one he had just left.

On time, the submarine surfaced and sent out a small boat Without ceremony, Louis climbed unsteadily aboard the submarine and was guided below. The captain gave orders and the submarine submerged before

Louis was welcomed aboard.

All his senses were being challenged. The cramped accommodation. The airless unpleasant diesel smell. The lack of windows. The odd reverberating sounds. The unfamiliar taste of the sweet milky tea which was given to him. A crew member smiled sympathetically.

"Come with me, I suggest you lie down in this bunk and try to sleep. It's all a bit unnerving at first." Louis was used to fishing boats, but this wasn't natural!

Louis was relieved when the captain told him that he was to be transferred to a frigate after a few hours, because the submarine had been given other duties.

As promised, Louis was transferred later that afternoon.

England again!

On arrival at Portsmouth, he was escorted ashore, to be greeted by two naval officers and taken to an interview room.

The senior officer addressed him abruptly.

"OK ... Who are you, and what happened to our man?"

Louis explained that he was working, with a Polish officer, for the Free French in Saint Jean de Luz. His colleague had made arrangements for a British officer to be collected by the cemetery and delivered by boat to another boat, for transfer to a submarine in open waters. The British officer had urgent secret information to take to England. *"Unfortunately, we were intercepted ... My colleague was shot dead, and also the British officer and his guide ... However, before he died, the British officer gave me this envelope, instructing me to take his place and deliver it to the British authorities. I have done what he asked!"*

"You have, indeed, done what he asked. Thank you. I will arrange for your transport to the Free French HQ and commend you for your brave achievements. This envelope will be delivered immediately to the War Office."

"Thank you sir!" replied Louis, *"But I'm exhausted and, before I go to my HQ, I would like a meal, a bath, some sleep and some clean clothes."*

"Of course!" He instructed his junior officer to look after Louis's needs and to arrange transport for the following morning.

And so, in a chauffeur-driven car, an invigorated Louis arrived at HQ to be presented to a very senior officer. He was debriefed, and officially given the rank of lieutenant.

In confidence, he was told the Free French were working with a British special operations group, based near Falmouth. The intention was to use a fishing boat which came from the Île de Sein for clandestine missions off Finistère's coast.

"The boat is being renovated and fitted with a more powerful engine. Two young brothers from the island have volunteered to crew the boat, under an experienced skipper. The boat will be based in Falmouth ... Will you be its skipper?"

"Yes sir ... willingly!"

"Excellent! The boat and its crew will be ready for collection, from Weymouth, in ten days' time. That gives you an opportunity to spend some time with your family in Penryn. We will contact you there!"

*

It was still May 1943 when Louis arrived back in Falmouth and went to Penryn harbour, where he saw the familiar Tanet boat at anchor. He went up the steep cobbled street and stopped at the cottage door. He knocked loudly on the door and shouted, *"This is the Customs ... Open up!"*

The door opened ... Josse and Paul filled the small doorway.

"Louis ... My God! Welcome home, stranger!"

The three joined in a three-man bear hug and went inside.

They talked, laughed and joked incessantly, trying to update each other on the missing time, including how Alan and Lena were settling in to farm life.

He agreed with the brother's revised financial arrangement that he, like Alan, was only due a half share in the boat while he wasn't a crew member. Louis also explained that he would be skippering another fishing boat, which would be based in Falmouth.

The following day, Josse and Paul went out on a fishing trip, while Louis called on Alan and Lena at the farm. Louis was impressed with the way Alan and Lena had settled in to farming, and the farmhouse was so homely. On listening to an edited version of his story,

Alan and Lena were so proud of their hero. Louis explained that, in just over a week's time, with the help of two lads from the Île de Sein, he would be skippering another fishing boat. Unfortunately, no accommodation had been arranged for them.

Lena promised to have a word with Alice, her 'honorary mother' in town.

She had a spare room, and would probably appreciate the company.

The army was busy everywhere, involving the local councillors and land owners, planning, what they called 'Operation Bolero', the preparation for accommodation and camp sites for a massive invasion of US military, with their equipment, including landing crafts, tanks, big guns, trucks and jeeps.

Amid this confusion, Louis successfully organised a mooring for the boat, and Alice agreed to take in the two lads. Louis then went to Weymouth and familiarised himself with the fishing boat and its young crew. He took them into town to buy provisions for a week's sea trials, on the way to Falmouth.

Louis and his young crew managed to establish themselves just in time, before thousands upon thousands of American troops noisily arrived and occupied every available corner they could find. New slipways were built and roads were widened to allow for their giant machinery.

Many locals moaned about being crushed by the swarms of brash noisy soldiers, but admitted, grudgingly, that here were allies, preparing to help the

British in a massive invasion of France and gain retribution against the Nazis, who were frequently bombing Falmouth.

Louis arranged with HQ that the boat would be used for fishing, in the normal way, but he had to report to them at least once a week, and be available for immediate instructions. Then, in August, he was given detailed instructions to rendezvous, at night, with another boat, at coordinates South-west of the Île de Sein, where he was to pick up three commandos after a raid in a major port.

He approached from due west and made the agreed signal … First time no response! Louis checked his watch and after two minutes … repeated the signal … He scoured the horizon, but nothing … a tiny signal came back from a little further south than expected. He headed closer and briefly flashed again … At last, an outline of the other boat! … The sea was calm, so the two boats came together and three camouflaged men silently jumped aboard.

"Merci, Bon voyage et Bonne chance! Et vous aussi!" and the boats parted.

The commandos were welcomed aboard with hot drinks, food and dry clothes.

Louis asked, in French, *"Was your mission a success?"*

"More or less!" was the guarded reply, also in French.

As dawn came up over Falmouth's Carrick Roads channel, they moored up temporarily alongside a naval launch and Louis escorted his passengers onto the other vessel.

"We'll take these gentlemen ashore and contact you later! ... Well done, Thank you!"

Louis then took his boat to its moorings. The lads went off to their new home at Alice's house, and Lewis crashed out on one of the bunks. Before the morning was out, a naval lieutenant came to the boat and escorted Louis to a bungalow outside of town for a short debriefing.

Several times, over the winter of 1943/44, Louis repeated his trips to Finistère, either collecting or delivering commandos or agents. Their reconnaissance missions helped the planning of the D-Day invasion in June 1944.

*

In November, 1944, Louis took the boat to the Île de Sein and returned the two lads to their parents. He found out which family owned the boat and returned it to them, suggesting that the two brothers continue as crew members. Several senior members of the family, and the two brothers, ferried Louis to Audierne.

The Alonso boat was in the harbour ... Lewis called out to his father, Matias, and the pair clung to each other, not wanting to let go, but, still clinging to each other, they staggered, like a couple of drunks, to the cottage. Maria threw her arms around her son, as they made a tearful reunion. So relieved they were all safe.

"But what about Alan and Lena, and Josse and Paul?"

"They are all well and send their love, but here is a

letter from Alan and Lena!" Maria opened it, read a little, and let out a squeal of delight. *"Did you know Lena is going to have a baby?"*

"No! When is it due?"

"In summer, next year!"

"Fantastic! I didn't know!"

After Maria had read the letter out loud, Louis asked about Corentin and Mavis. Matias replied that Corentin had been losing weight and was too weak to go fishing, so he now helped Mavis doing light duties on the farm and they were depending on a farmhand and a neighbour to work the fields.

Louis gave a very brief account of his adventures, and an update on Alan and Lena and the Tanet brothers in Penryn.

When Louis visited the farm, they were delighted that he was safe and wanted to know about the others. Louis handed Mavis a letter from Alan and Lena. She read it out loud and reached for a chair when she read that Lena was pregnant. She read on and thanked God that her sons were thriving in Penryn.

"Will they all be coming home?"

"I don't know ... At the moment, they are very happy with their new lives in England ... I think Alan and Lena will stay, but the boys may come back home, to look after you both."

Louis re-established himself at the cottage and rejoined Matias as mate on the Alonso boat.

*

In December, there was a surprise arrival in

Audierne. The Tanet boat tied up at the harbourside. Louis had seen them approach and was waiting on the quay to greet them. Impatiently, he went on board and was surprised to see that Lena and Alan were also there.

"What's this all about? Have you come for Christmas?"

"All in good time!" replied Josse.

From the cottage, Matias had also seen their arrival and brought Maria. They too went on board to welcome the 'children'.

Once the initial hubbub had died down, Josse suggested that all of them go to the farm, as one, and tell their stories together.

Mavis shouted excitedly to Corentin, *"Look who's coming up the lane! ... It's the whole family!"*

Soon, they were crowded around the table, with a cider jug being passed from one to another, and refilled.

Alan and Lena had the biggest story ... Lena was in the early months of her pregnancy. She was happy and healthy and Alan was very protective, but they delighted their parents with the news that they were in Audierne to stay. They had ended their tenancy of the farm in Penryn and both wanted to help run the Tanet farm in Audierne, now that they had some practical experience. Lena was concerned about her father's health and wanted to help look after him.

The news from Josse and Paul was mixed. Disappointing for the family, but they were extremely happy with their lives in Penryn. They had been welcomed as part of the community and had made many friends there.

Alice, who Lena had nicknamed 'Honorary Mother', had invited the boys to leave their rented cottage and make their home with her. (In 1945, she secretly made a will, leaving everything, including the house, to Josse and Paul) … After Christmas, Josse and Paul would return to Penryn, but promised to make occasional trips to Audierne.

While the women were preparing a celebratory meal, the men discussed the boats and came to a unanimous agreement that Josse and Paul would now be the sole owners of the Tanet boat. It was suggested that ownership of the Alonso boat should be shared between Louis and Alan, but Alan, (with Lena's blessing), declined and Louis was appointed the sole owner. Corentin, (with Mavis's blessing), passed ownership of the farm to Alan and Lena jointly. They all agreed that the future of the family was assured.

In the years that followed, Louis was awarded the Légion d'Honneur for his service to France, as a foreign national, living in France.

In 1973, before Josse and Paul retired, the towns of Penryn and Audierne were established as Twin Towns and both men proudly contributed their efforts.

16. NORFOLK

When the war ended in 1945, Rosa was fourteen and still attending school.

In March 1946, when Mary and her girls returned to London to stay with Mary's aunt, Rosa was sad to lose her evacuee sisters.

Jane took up a management role with Norfolk hospital board while Leo continued to work hard studying medicine and became an operating theatre nurse in a large hospital.

In Spain, during Franco's dictatorship, there was economic hardship and a harsh repression of the people. Leo heard nothing of his Spanish family and because mail in Spain was being censored, he was reluctant to make any attempt to contact them in case it would have serious repercussions.

Although Eric, Jane's father, had retired in 1940 at the age of 70, he occasionally lent a hand at the surgery until 1945 when his heart was telling him to slow down. In May, 1946, his heart finally gave up one night and the family was left with a painful void.

In the early summer of 1947, Rosa, now 16, was maturing into a beautiful slim young woman. She had large green dancing eyes, reflecting her bright cheerful friendly manner. Her jet-black hair was cut in a bob to frame her attractive face. She carried her petite body gracefully and seemed to be constantly on the move, investigating something or chatting animatedly with friends.

She enjoyed athletics and, during the school's annual sports day, 17-year- old Pete Denby complimented her on her victory in one of the races.

Pete, in the year above Rosa, was tall and looked muscular but slim. He had a handsome face, black hair and hazel eyes. His easy smile and relaxed manner invited casual conversation as the two chatted between their various events.

During the school holidays, the two became good friends and went on cycle runs, sometimes with other friends and sometimes just the two of them. Occasionally, they went to the cinema and, slowly, they accepted being called girlfriend and boyfriend.

Their romance developed and continued at the end of the following school year, after Pete had left school.

He could have been called up for National Service when he left school, but because farm workers had been given exemption from National Service, his father advised him to come and work on the farm for a year and so delay going to the army until he was 19.

His reason was that Pete would benefit from being a year older and consequently avoid being one of the more vulnerable younger soldiers. Pete accepted his Dad's suggestion and began working on the farm.

As farm and school work permitted, they would go on cycle runs together or see a film. However, although they were fond of each other, as summer 1949 approached, they knew that both of them were going to have new lives calling them away from each other ... Rosa wanted to study anatomy and physiology at university and Pete's National Service was looming.

In July, Pete volunteered for the infantry and left for his initial training. In autumn, Rosa enrolled in Norwich University. They promised to write to each other every week, and although they often thought of each other, their new lives created a massive distraction and their letters became few and far between.

Rosa shared a flat with two other medical students, Jenny and Pat, and the three enjoyed life, whilst doing little more than the fundamental requirements demanded by the course tutors.

However, thanks to Jane's influence in the hospital, Rosa was allowed to help doctors and patients by assisting in the use of physical therapy, which one or two of the doctors were studying as a new science to help the recovery of patients suffering from limited mobility.

*

In 1949, Rosa spent her Christmas break at home with Jane, Leo and her grandmother, Grace.

Christmas followed the family tradition, with a visit from her Aunt Marian, Uncle George and her cousins Barbara, Simon and David. They came for Christmas Eve and stayed until Boxing Day.

Despite her 71 years, Grace presided over the festivities as usual, although, now, Jane and Marian did most of the work.

In the privacy of their bedroom, Rosa and Barbara swapped intimate experiences of their student lives away from home, while, as usual, they kept the boys at bay.

Simon and David insisted on hearing stories from Leo, but, after a while, George sent them outside so he could have his own time with Leo.

Once alone with Leo, George explained that Simon, now 17, had been helping him on the farm and how he was keenly interested in a farming career. After school, Simon would hopefully go to college or university and obtain a suitable qualification. This, of course would give him exemption from National Service.

George added, *"We have heard about Rosa's boyfriend, but we have advised Simon that **his** future lies in the farm and it would be better if he concentrates fully on studying."*

On Boxing Day morning, David rushed into the lounge. *"There's a soldier coming up the drive!"*

Leo welcomed him, *"You must be Pete Denby!"*

"Yessir!" was the brief reply.

"How's army life, Pete?"

"OK, but the food's awful!" He looked up, as he saw Rosa coming down the stairs, coloured slightly, and gave a big smile.

"Pete! What a lovely surprise!"

By now, the whole family had gathered in the hall to see who had arrived.

Jane put a hand on Pete's arm, *"Merry Christmas Pete! The uniform suits you!"* She looked at the family and waved her hands in the direction of the lounge.

"We're crowding Rosa's visitor. Back into the lounge, the lot of you! Rosa! Introduce Pete to Barbara! The three of you should go upstairs. You don't need this audience."

"Thanks, Mum!" as Rosa led Pete and Barbara upstairs.

Pete told the girls of his first six weeks 'square bashing' and how the less fit and younger members of his group had been subjected to bullying. He was thankful that his year of working on the farm had prepared him for the hard physical life of the army, but felt that any attempts to display initiative were disappointingly treated as resistance to authority.

Rosa was impressed, but felt that Pete had changed.

He seemed older and more distant, even when Barbara left the room on some pretext. He didn't have that relaxed warm smile.

Rosa didn't want to tell him of the freedom she was experiencing at university. It would be like teasing a poor hungry person by describing her enjoyment of good food and leisure.

Jane called from the foot of the stairs, *"Would Pete like to join us for lunch?"*

Rosa looked at him enquiringly …

Pete went to the door and looked down the stairs, *"No thanks, Mrs Garcia. I told my Mum and Dad I would be home for lunch."*

"Are you sure?"

"Yes thanks!"

Shortly after, Pete said goodbye to everybody, then Rosa pecked him on the cheek, wished him good luck, and waved to him as he walked down the drive.

*

Barbara led Rosa back to their bedroom, clearly intending to talk about Pete and his visit, but Simon followed them saying,

"Shame he went! I wanted to find out what National Service is like!"

Rosa looked at him with a serious expression, *"Stick to farming Simon ... It's what you want, isn't it? One day the farm will be yours ... Anyway, National Service will change you. Avoid it if you can!"*

"You sound like my Dad!" replied Simon as he closed the door.

Barbara could see that Rosa didn't want to talk about it, so reverted to chatting about university life and flat sharing with other girls. *(Sorry! Other Young Women!)*

After Christmas, Rosa went back to her university life ... working hard, and playing hard when she and her flat mates went out on the town. She would receive an occasional letter from Pete, but they were becoming more infrequent.

Summer holidays signalled the end of her first year at university. Occasionally, she would visit her cousin Barbara, or Barbara would come and stay with her, but, during the holidays, Rosa missed the hectic life with her flat mates.

*

A few days after returning to university for her

second year, Rosa received a brief note from Pete, saying that he was being sent to Korea with a large contingent of British troops. He seemed excited to be part of a large military action. "*Action at last*", he said!

Rosa and her flat mates, Jenny and Pat, had to take their second year more seriously. The work was more challenging and there was more pressure from the tutors … Fortunately, they supported each other's studies in the flat and only went out at weekends … Christmas 1950 came and went! … Meanwhile news of fighting in Korea was grim, with reports of serious British casualties being inflicted, not only by North Koreans and Chinese, but even by a misguided US air attack.

Rosa and Jenny decided to stay on in the flat for the Easter holidays, while Pat went to visit her parents. One night, at a local dance hall, they joined a little group of engineering students. Rosa was attracted to one of them.

Colin Watson was the comedian in the group. He and his friends were studying for a degree in agricultural engineering. He had unruly fair hair, a rugged face with square jaw. A quick wit, deep voice and infectious laugh. When they danced, Rosa's ear was level with Colin's shoulder. He was taller, but comfortably taller than she was. *(She liked that!)* He was a good dancer too!

In his four-door Austin Devon, Colin drove Rosa and Jenny back to the flat. The girls were impressed … with Colin and Rosa in the front and Jenny in the back with Colin's friend, Don. They laughed and joked into the early hours before Colin and Don left the girls to happily chat over a most enjoyable evening with two great guys.

The following two or three weekends, they went out as a foursome, but Jenny cooled-off towards Don, then Colin and Rosa became closer.

Towards the end of April, 1951, news headlines described a fierce battle at the Imjin River in Korea … Early in May, after several telephone calls to Pete's parents, Rosa heard that Pete had been killed, at the age of 21, with many other brave British soldiers.

After another year at university, Rosa graduated with a degree in anatomy and physiology and Colin obtained a degree in Agricultural Engineering.

Rosa found a job in Norwich hospital and began helping in the establishment of a new Physiotherapy department.

Colin continued to help his father in his well-established farm machinery business near Thetford … Colin helped to develop, assemble and demonstrate new farm machinery. Colin's father was able to spend more time in importing and exporting farm machinery and Colin also learned more about the business finance.

Because Rosa and Colin were both developing their separate careers, their limited time with each other became more precious and they wanted to spend more time together, so, the pair were engaged shortly after the Coronation in June 1953.

In April, 1954, Colin's father bought them an old, dilapidated vicarage for the couple to restore. It took them a year to get planning permission and complete the extension, which still left them with a great deal of work to finish the interior and make the garden acceptable …

Finally, in April 1956, they were married and officially moved into their fully renovated home. Rose now used the name Rosa García Watson.

To Rosa and Colin – A son

On 22nd May 1958, Rosa gave birth to Robert García Watson and decided to give up her full-time job and only do occasional relief work until Robert was settled in school.

However, when Robert was only four years old, being a full-time mother was not enough for Rosa and she wanted to go back to work, even if it was only three days a week. Grace, Rosa's grandma, volunteered to look after him if Rose wanted to go back to work. However, Grace was now 83 and an exuberant four-year-old like Robert would have been too much for her.

Rosa's mother and father, were still working, so Rosa had to wait until Robert started school the following year, before returning to full-time work.

Leo and Jane had become very proud grandparents and Leo wanted to share the news with his mother, who was now a great grandmother and, of course, José, Rosa's Spanish father, was now a grandfather.

Jane reminded Leo that, in Spain, his mother would be 77 and José would be 53. *"Would you like us to take Rosa and Robert to see your family? Spain has opened up to tourists now! What do you say?"*

After a family discussion, it was decided that it would

be better to start with a letter from Leo to Rosa's Spanish father. He should explain that they had not written earlier because of the political repression in Spain. They thought that possible censorship could have resulted in persecution of the family. However, at last, it would seem the cause for fear had passed.

The letter should enquire about the family in Spain and tell José about Rosa, her husband, Colin, and their son Robert … and their full and happy family life in England with Leo, Jane and her family.

In the end, Rosa and Leo each wrote a letter and enclosed photographs.

However, it was October by the time they each received a reply from José, giving them a family update.

Sadly, both Rosa's grandmothers, Teresa and Alicia, died in 1954.

Rosa´s father, José, had remarried in 1947 and two years later, his wife had given birth to a son, named Eduardo, after José's father. José's family vineyard was still doing well!

Ana, (Leo's bar assistant), now did delivery rounds in the old van, but, in addition to selling goats-milk and cheese, she now sold eggs and home-made bread for selected clients. Miguel, Ana's nephew, was now married, with two children and he and his wife managed the farm with the guidance and assistance of Ana.

Leo and Rosa read and reread the letters and translated them for the rest of the family. The family sympathetically supported Leo and Rosa in their decision not to go to Spain. They all felt that, with the passage of time, each branch of the family was successfully making its own way. (It was best not to live in the past, but to savour the present and prepare for a happy road ahead).

As Robert grew up, he loved to sit with Colin on a tractor or any other big machine. Rosa thought it was too dangerous for a little boy, but took comfort in the knowledge that Colin supervised him closely and patiently.

In May 1963, at 'The Old Vicarage', Rosa and Colin's home, Robert had his fifth birthday party. In the garden, he and his friends raced around on bicycles, while the adults relaxed in the sun.

Later, back at their own house, Leo and Jane were reminiscing ... It was just over a year since Grace, Jane's mum, had died at the age of 83.

Leo and Jane had inherited the house and, in addition, a significant trust fund had been set up for her brother, George.

Because Robert was starting school and Rosa wanted to go back to work, Jane retired in September and agreed to collect Robert from school and look after him until Rosa finished work. The following year, Leo also retired, at the age of sixty, and they enjoyed the time now spent with their grandson.

Rosa threw herself into her work at the hospital and became one of the unsung developers in the new science of Physiotherapy. Indeed, she became a specialist in the new techniques of increasing patients' mobility and improving their quality of life.

During Robert's school years, he showed more interest in practical work than in academic studies. He enjoyed cycling, running, rugby and judo.

His mother's and his grandfather's efforts to teach him Spanish were met with some resistance, but he did gain a basic knowledge, not only of the language, but also of what was happening in Spain … Franco had died in 1975. Prince Juan Carlos had become king and was left to deal with the challenges of democracy.

In 1978, Leo received a letter from José, telling him that Ana had passed away quietly in her sleep. He enclosed a letter from Ana, saying how much she had loved Leo and how Teresa, his mother, had taken her into the family as though she was Leo's widow. When Teresa died, Ana's grief was immense, but Teresa had passed on the farm to her with instructions to take care of it in loving memory of her adopted mother-in- law.

Leo sent a letter of condolence to Ana's nephew, Miguel, confirmed that Miguel was now the owner of the farm, and wished him and his family… success and happiness for the future.

On leaving school at the age of 18, Robert started work as a trainee mechanic on Colin's agricultural machines. He did not want to go to university, but took an engineering technician course at the local college.

On his twenty-first birthday, he was promoted to salesman, but a year later, after general restlessness and poor performance, he volunteered for the paratroopers, hoping for more action in his life.

The family were shocked and horrified at the thought

of him joining the army and possibly going into a war zone ... Rosa couldn't help but think of how her boyfriend had been killed in Korea, but they were unable to change Robert's mind.

After initial selection and training, Robert was posted to Northern Ireland, followed by a brief assignment in Belize. Then in 1982, he saw action in the Falklands war.

In the winter of 1984, Robert's uncle George died, after contracting pleurisy which developed into pneumonia.

Marian tried to maintain her usual extrovert buoyant manner, but couldn't hide her grief. One morning, the following spring, she failed to answer her daughter's daily 'phone call.

Early in 1987, Leo received a letter from Miguel, telling of the death of Rosa's natural father, José.

*

Later in 1987, after seven years' service, having reached the rank of sergeant, Robert left the army.

Rosa and Colin organised a big 'Welcome Home' party at their home in the old vicarage. They were delighted to have him home again, without injury.

Robert enjoyed his return to civilian life and went back to work as a salesman for his father.

The following Easter, Robert was helping Colin to modify a massive new machine ... They were on their own, working in the yard ... Rosa was at work and Colin's new apprentice was at college ... Colin clambered onto an outrigger, ignoring Robert's warning that the metal was still damp from the overnight dew. *"Let me do that, Dad!"*

"I'm all right!" came back Colin's exasperated reply.

Then he slipped, falling backwards, with his lower back hitting a support arm ...

His left foot struck a cutting blade before he fell clear of the machine..He yelled as he landed on his back on the hard ground. Blood began to pour from his calf. Colin was breathing, but his pulse was feint ... Robert felt that time was of the essence and didn't want his Dad to die on the concrete floor of the yard whilst waiting for an ambulance. He planned to put Colin in the minibus and take him to the hospital himself!

In the army, Robert had seen terrible injuries, but had been trained to deal with them without delay ... He removed his belt and put a tourniquet on Colin's leg ... He was worried about what damage may have been done to his Dad's back or neck, so had to be extremely careful when moving him.

Robert went to the barn to see what he could use as a stretcher. Against one wall, was an old kitchen worktop ... *(That would do!)* He placed the worktop beside Colin, as close as he could. Then, very carefully, taking care not to cause further damage to Colin's back, he slid Colin onto the improvised stretcher.

Single-handedly, he had to get Colin, from ground level, into the minibus, but if he put one end of the stretcher into the minibus, while the other end was on the ground, Colin could slide down the stretcher onto the ground. *(That would be disastrous!)*

Robert kept talking to Colin and making sure he was still awake. *"Let's get this small crate under the stretcher below your feet ... Good ... That's not too high!"*

Next, so that Colin's head was just above the level of the minibus floor, he slid a larger crate under the stretcher below Colin's shoulders ... *(The stretcher was now at a shallow angle, with Colin's head higher than his feet).*

The company minibus was in the yard. (The rear seats had been removed some time ago). He opened the tailgate, and reversed the vehicle close to Colin's head ... Robert returned to the stretcher by Colin's feet, lifted it and kicked away the small crate before gently pushing the stretcher into the van.

"There you are, Dad, let me cover you with this old blanket and put this rolled-up jacket under your head ... We can't have you shivering, can we?"

As he drove off, he called the police on his mobile, explained that he needed a police escort to the hospital emergency bay ... His passenger has a severed blood vessel and may have a broken back ... He told them where he was and the route he intended to take WITHOUT JOLTING HIS PASSENGER!

He stayed on his mobile and gave them the additional details they needed.

He was still several miles from the hospital when he saw a police car, with its blue lights flashing. Robert flashed his lights and tucked in behind the police car as it moved off. Police, on two motorbikes alternated ahead of them, controlling road junctions, so that they didn't have to stop until they arrived at the emergency entrance of the hospital.

Two attendants in white jackets and trousers opened the tailgate and, under Robert's supervision, took out the improvised stretcher and Colin.

With their patient still on the worktop, they put him on a trolley and whisked him down a corridor to the emergency area. Robert was right behind them and briefed the duty doctor about the accident, before Colin was taken for examination and initial treatment.

A policeman spoke to Robert, *"We have moved your van away from the ambulance parking area ... You left your keys in the ignition"*. *"Here, take them!"* he added, as he put the keys in Robert's hand.

Robert thanked him and then the two discussed what had happened, so that a formal report could be completed.

The policeman complimented Robert on the way he had dealt with the accident and, before saying goodbye, wished Colin a speedy recovery.

After a long wait, Robert was informed by the doctor that Colin had received some minor surgery on his calf, that a tendon had been fractured and that his back injury wasn't serious, but would need physiotherapy ... Colin would be admitted for a couple of days!

Robert said that his mother, Colin's wife, was a resident physiotherapist... that she was currently on duty ... *"Would you please call her to come here ... I want to give her the news gently."*

"Oh, you mean Rosa Watson! Certainly, I'll call her. Just wait there!"

Rosa soon appeared. *"What's wrong ... Are you OK?"*

"Yes, Mum, Dad's fine but he fell off some machinery ... He's hurt his back and his foot ... He's in there ... Have a word with the doctor!"

A little later, Rosa returned, *"They've just bandaged your dad's foot, rather than putting it in plaster, because they want to change the dressing on the cut ... After he has rested for a couple of days, they'll refer him to me for physiotherapy ...*

They said you didn't call an ambulance, but brought him in on a kitchen worktop! ... What's that all about?"

Robert explained, *"It was faster that way, and he wasn't left on the yard floor, waiting for an ambulance to arrive ... If I had spent time on the phone, calling the emergency services, then I couldn't have given Dad the attention he needed ...*

"So I delayed asking for a police escort until I was actually driving Dad here ... I could do that without extending the time it would take to get medical help for him."

"When you put it that way," replied Rosa, *"I'm sure that was best. I'm proud of you ... Very few people could have handled an emergency like that on their own, without panicking!"*

Colin was soon released from hospital, but Rosa and Robert were not surprised when he proved to be a difficult patient.

Rosa insisted that he followed the exercise

programme she had given him and not strain his back. Colin, however, was impatient to return to managing the business and, grudgingly, had no alternative but to allow Robert to act on his behalf.

Rosa reminded him, *"You used to dream of Robert following in your footsteps one day by taking over the business and allowing you to retire!"*

Colin grunted, *"Yes, but I'm only 61 and not ready for it yet!"*

"Yes, but I am!" replied Rosa.

"I would like both of us to retire, and that will give Robert a chance to show his metal!" replied Rosa.

*

By summer, 1989, Colin was back in action again and pleased to hear customers teasing him by asking if things would go back to the old 'rustic' way again or, some would simply praise Robert for his enthusiasm.

Robert was on a night out, with a few friends in a bar in Cambridge. At another table, there were three young women chatting happily and Robert kept looking at the most attractive one.

Her long chestnut hair danced about her tanned face from which her brown eyes sparkled. She wore an elegant short body-hugging black silk dress which showed off her petite slim figure.

Her vivacious enthusiasm was infecting her friends.

Robert kept glancing at her and, a couple of times, saw her eyes briefly flash in his direction, although she didn't alter the flow of animated conversation with her friends.

Robert was on his way to the bar to fetch a round of drinks and, as he passed the other table, he couldn't resist another glance at her.

She stood up and confronted him, saying quietly, almost secretively,

"Why do you keep staring at me?"

(Her forehead was level with his chin) ... Robert looked down into her eyes, He smiled, and quietly replied, *"Sorry, I meant no offence, but glancing furtively at you wasn't enough ... I couldn't help but let each glance take a little longer than the previous one."* He paused and added, *"Please let me talk to you before you leave!"*

She glanced at him thoughtfully and slowly sat down, while her friends looked on curiously.

Robert returned to his friends while thinking, 'Nice legs too!' He put the drinks on the table ... *"Do you know her?"*

"Not yet!" replied Robert.

Conspiratorially, his friends left Robert at the table when they left ... A little later, HER friends said goodbye and Robert moved to the other table.

"Hello, I'm Robert, Thanks for staying!"

"Hi, I'm Helen ... My friends are outside ... I can't keep them waiting for long!"

However, after ten minutes or so, Helen went outside to confirm that her friends were no longer waiting.

She then returned to Robert and the two of them exchanged more personal details and agreed to meet each other a few days later. Robert then drove her home and they kissed briefly at the entrance to her apartment block.

Their romance deepened and three or four months later, Robert bought a cottage in a small village within commuting distance from Cambridge. Then, on 31st March, 1990, they were married in the village church. It was a modest affair, followed by a meal in a nearby hotel.

The couple kept their same jobs, with Helen continuing as an accountant in Cambridge and Robert progressively taking over the business from his father.

Although Helen wanted children, Robert was quietly content that they had none and neither wanted to adopt any.

In April 1991, Rosa retired, at the age of 60, to look after her ageing parents … In December, 1991, Leo died at the age of 87 and, the following summer, Jane died at the age of 80 … Rosa inherited the house but sold it three months later. Colin then retired, at the age of 65, and he had a month's summer holiday with Rosa on the Costa del Sol.

*

In March 1996, to celebrate their six happy years of marriage, Robert arranged a romantic weekend in Paris. He booked a show, a river boat tour and a meal in a top restaurant.

They returned to their weekday routine where Helen would finish work in Cambridge at about 5.00pm and Robert a little earlier. This allowed Robert to meet Helen when her train arrived at their local station.

However, later that year, on Monday 14th July 1996, Robert waited for Helen at the station. The train came in and left, but Helen didn't show. He was worried, but hoped she had simply missed her train ... It had happened before, albeit only twice in six years! ... So he waited for the next train, over an hour later ...

When the train came in, he was waiting on the platform ... The train left and he felt an ominous void in the pit of his stomach ... A well-dressed middle-aged man approached him.

"Are you Robert Watson?"

"Yes, what's happened?"

"Helen went out for a sandwich at lunchtime ... We heard tyres screeching, followed by shouting and screaming. A car had hit Helen on a pedestrian crossing, then drove off immediately! A colleague saw it happen and went to help, but Helen was dead ... It was so fast, at least she didn't suffer for long!

"The police arrived within minutes and an ambulance took her to hospital. Her colleague was in shock and the ambulance took her too.

"I am Jon Harding, a fellow partner at the practice, I'll stay with you tonight until a relative can be with you."

Robert couldn't speak ... He nodded agreement ... Jon bundled Robert into the passenger seat and drove, following Robert's sobbing directions, to the cottage where Robert collapsed into a sofa chair and silently allowed tears to fall onto his shaking body.

Jon fed Robert with tea and whisky until he finally fell asleep on the sofa chair. Jon then fell asleep on the other sofa chair and wakened up just after dawn to find Robert standing in the kitchen with a mug of tea in his hand.

"Thanks for bringing me home! I'm going to Cambridge ... I want to see the police ... find out what they're doing to find the bastard Have Helen's parents been told? . I need to tell MY mother and father. There's a train in an hour's time. You can have something to eat at the station .I'm ready to go when you are!"

Jon saw the determination in Robert's face. *"Err ... Yes OK ... I'll have a quick wash first!"*

When they boarded the train, Jon regretted drinking the vending machine coffee in the station foyer and looked forward to reaching home and his personal comforts.

Once in Cambridge, Jon drove Robert to the police station where they parted company.

The police were sympathetic. They explained that, yesterday afternoon, they had attended a road traffic accident where a car had crashed into a bollard ... The driver reeked of alcohol and admitted to hitting a woman on a pedestrian crossing. He was being held in custody.

Robert was allowed to phone Helen's father and then phoned Colin ... Colin said he would come and fetch him and bring him home, where, together, they could tell his mother.

The funeral was held in Cambridge and, the mourners not only included Helen and Robert's families and friends, but also all the staff from the accounting practice came to pay their respects.

After the funeral, the accounting partners held a memorial buffet which families and friends also attended.

Once home, in the solitude of the cottage and his memories of Helen, Robert fell asleep over an empty bottle of whisky.

The following morning, he never heard Rosa and Colin at the front door, nor did he hear them noisily enter through the kitchen door. *"Come on son, you're coming home with us for a while!"*

"But I'll be"

"No buts, we'll come back here every day until you're sorted!"

Progressively, Rosa helped Robert to clear the cottage and move back with her and Colin.

For the rest of that year, Robert's attention was directed towards selling the cottage and to the court case against Helen's killer.

Both Robert and Colin had lost enthusiasm for the business and sold it.

It took until April to sell Robert's cottage and for the judge to sentence Helen's killer to a long prison sentence. For Robert, anything short of a death sentence was too lenient, but that was the law!

Robert needed work, to get out of his constant fits of depression in which it was becoming more and more difficult to resist seeking solace in whisky.

Rosa encouraged him to use his bicycle, which was

still in the shed. He followed the advice and became fitter ... both physically and mentally.

However, late one afternoon in May 1997, Robert was driving near the old cottage and couldn't resist the impulse to go and look at it. He stopped opposite, but didn't get out of the car, then drove to the station, where he used to meet her.

He started dreaming of Helen and, almost in a trance, sat in the car and dozed off ... Waiting and Wishing.

He heard the train's special sound. Drew a breath, and sensed elation.

Then felt his heart begin to pound to know it's nearly at the station.

Now, shaken by the noise it made, it raced on past with a mighty roar.

Then the pain which does not fade. She's not outside the station door!

He heard a tapping on the glass ... A PC's voice ... I'm sure you knew,

Since the time you lost your lass, Trains, they too, just pass on through!

That incident was a wake-up call for Robert ... He soon found a driving job with a haulage company who were looking for drivers with an HGV licence for a regular run to and from Alicante. Ideally, they should have experience with large vehicles and an understanding of Spanish.

The company explained that they had experienced occasional problems on return trips when, on the French border, French farmers' unions had destroyed complete cargoes of fresh produce, while the Gendarmes simply looked on.

They were now changing the route to use the Portsmouth Bilbao ferry, so the route would be in three parts – East Anglia to Portsmouth: An overnight crossing to Bilbao: A direct run to Alicante, but sometimes, to companies further south than Alicante.

Robert pointed out that the law may require him to make an overnight stop in Spain. He could accept that, and the company agreed.

His first run was in July 1997.

The prospect of his new job suited Robert. He felt that his experience in the Paras had helped prepare him, not only for the physical and mental determination needed, but also, it had given him the ability to deal calmly with surprise events.

17. ROBERT RETURNS TO HIS SPANISH ROOTS

His main journeys were to Alicante to collect fresh horticultural produce and deliver it to a warehouse in East Anglia.

Sometimes, on his way to Alicante, he would collect a load in southern England and drop it off at the ferry terminal in Bilbao or at an agreed rest stop near Madrid. On his return journey, he would occasionally pick up a trailer near Madrid and leave it at a depot near Portsmouth.

He found the port authorities and Police or Guardia Civil to be helpful and they responded well to Robert's friendly but respectful way of talking to them. On his rest days in Alicante, Robert hired a car and explored the Southern Costa Blanca and the Mar Menor area of the Costa Cálida.

Most of the produce he took on his truck was brought on a supplier's truck from Huércal Overa, in the province of Almeria.

He struck up a friendship with the driver, who was a short, thick-set man in his early sixties, with a lived-in face, bulbous nose and a shock of silvery hair under a scruffy flat cap. He wore a stained short-sleeved blue T-shirt, baggy jeans, held up by a broad leather belt. In his open-toed sandals, his slow, flat footed gait accentuated his age.

At first, Robert had difficulty understanding Matias' Andaluz accent which was interspersed with the odd mispronounced English word or phrase.

It transpired that Matias' cousin owned the distribution company in Huércal Overa and Matias was one of only three drivers who collected produce from the growers and made deliveries to other distributors.

Whenever he could, Robert would go and visit Matias and his family, who encouraged him to relax and enjoy life.

Robert was now Roberto García Watson! When he was called that, it made him feel he had come back to his maternal family roots in Andalucía and his smile radiated warmth from within!

After his wife's tragic accident, Robert had sold his cottage in England and returned to his parents' home at the Old Vicarage in Norfolk.

One evening, after dinner, in November, 1997, Robert confided in them…

"You know, when I'm in Spain, I live each day as it comes … I don't keep looking back, I don't get depressed. What would you say if I rent a place in Almeria province and make that my home?"

Colin smiled at Robert *."Your mother and I have seen you come back to life and it makes us very happy indeed."*

Rosa joined in, *"Your dad and I are delighted that*

you're thinking about your future again, even if we won't see you so often!"

"*You still have a home here, son, whatever you do!"* added Colin.

In the following months, Robert continued with his same job, but explained to his employer that he would like to spend more time in Spain and, if possible, could his routes be planned to start with a full truck in Huércal Overa, where he has made contact with a new distributor, but otherwise still do the same journeys.

"*I'll give it some thought, but make no promises,"* replied his boss.

In March 1998, Robert found a furnished house to rent. It was a recently built two bedroomed mid-terraced house within easy walking distance from Huércal Overa's town centre. There was underground parking and it wasn't long before he was using it for an old second-hand car which he bought as a runabout.

He had heard that free Spanish classes were provided by the town hall and Robert attended when he could. He liked the class which was attended mainly by UK expats and he studied hard, whilst making new friends.

Robert loved football and used to help with an amateur team in Norfolk, so it wasn't long before his Spanish friends persuaded him to help with a local youth team. It gave him a new dimension to his social life and helped with his Spanish.

One day, Matias took Robert to meet his cousin, Vicente, at the packing and distribution warehouse. Matias looked a little smarter than usual, in his blue denim shirt tucked into a clean pair of jeans …

Vicente, in his early fifties, was younger than Matias. He was a little taller but of similar stature although less corpulent. Below his sparse black hair, his less bulbous nose was set in a tanned face with smooth complexion. He wore a check shirt, with sleeves half-rolled-up and blue jeans.

He approached Robert with a vigorous walk and began greeting him loudly in English from about four metres away.

"So you are the English friend of Matias! Hello Roberto! … I am pleased to meet you!"

"Likewise!" replied Robert as Vicente led them upstairs to his office which was on a mezzanine overlooking the open-plan warehouse. Matias excused himself and made his way to the garage.

"Roberto," began Vicente in a mixture of English and Spanish, *"Matias has told me that you work for an English transport company … You drive a truck with our produce from Alicante to Bilbao and to England … That you have mechanical experience with large vehicles, and you now live in Huércal Overa …*

"He also told me that you have asked your company if you could be based here in Huércal Overa, but they have not given you an answer … Is that correct?"

"Yes that's correct," replied Robert.

"Good!" continued Vicente. *"I wish to expand the transport part of my company … I have five medium sized trucks, two small ones, my 4 x 4 and a fork lift … I have three drivers, (Matias being one of them) and a*

mechanic ... The garage and workshop is at the back of the warehouse ... I will show you around shortly ... I am prepared to buy two long distance trucks, to establish direct deliveries to England and stop using the transport company in Alicante ...

"However, I need a working manager who can take full responsibility for what will become a separate transport company ... I understand you also have experience managing a farm machinery business ... If the position I have described would be of interest to you, we can discuss details later, so you can present me with a plan. Are you interested?"

"I am stunned ... and very interested!"

Vicente then took Robert on a tour of the garage, (with Matias in tow). Robert silently inspected each vehicle thoroughly under the watchful eyes of Vicente and Matias.

Robert asked the mechanic some questions about the maintenance of the vehicles and what records were kept.

He briefly inspected the garage office, storeroom and equipment before the trio returned to Vicente's office.

Once there, he opened the door into the general office.

"Maria! I would like you to meet Roberto García Watson who is interested in our transport section."

"Roberto, let me introduce you to Maria Mendoza, our Office Manager, who is also my Finance Manager. Nothing worthwhile happens here without Maria approving it!"

"I wish!" she replied jovially and moved towards Robert. *"I am pleased to meet you!"*

They shook hands as Robert acknowledged her.

They both saw something interesting in each other and Vicente noticed that the handshaking lasted a little longer than usual … Maria took a small step backwards. *"Vicente! How can I help?"*

Vicente smiled … *"I would like you to help Roberto to produce a detailed proposal of how to develop the transport section into a separate company operating direct deliveries to Bilbao and England."*

"Interesting ... OK!" she replied, looking enquiringly at Robert, who nodded back.

"Is a month enough time for you both?" asked Vicente.

"I don't know, but, for now, let's say YES," Roberto replied and looked at Maria, *"Do you agree, Maria?"*

"Why not!" was her reply, *"I'll clear the storeroom at the back of the office and Roberto can use that ... Give me until next Tuesday and we'll be ready for you Roberto!"*

Robert thanked Vicente and looked admiringly at Maria, *"I am looking forward to working with you!"* Then, as he left. *"Thank you both ... I'll see you next Tuesday!"*

He found Matias in the garage and gave him a manly hug, patting his back, *"You old schemer!"* Matias didn't know what a schemer was, but he had made his friend happy so he was content!

Robert telephoned his boss, saying that he needed a month's holiday … With reluctance, the boss agreed.

Early the following Tuesday, Robert showered, put

on a fresh white shirt and formal trousers. He paused in front of the mirror, *"Ready for inspection!"* and left for the warehouse.

Maria, too, was ready for inspection … She wore a white shirt/blouse with open collar, revealing a black neckband with gold pendant. Her black snug-fitting jeans were tucked into her high-heeled leather boots.

Maria showed Robert into the little back office, which had a window overlooking the warehouse. Near the window, there was a table and four chairs. At the other end of the room, there was a cupboard, plus a neat stack of boxes. On the desk was a small assortment of stationery. *"Tomorrow, you will have a telephone! I suggest you spend the morning in the garage and we have a talk over lunch at two o'clock … OK?"*

"OK!" agreed Robert and, after a few minutes, he went to the garage. The mechanic was working on one of the large trucks but acknowledged Robert's greeting …

Robert soon ascertained that, of the five large trucks, two were about three years old, two, about five years old and one, even older. The old one was permanently parked outside and used for spare parts. The two small tired-looking vehicles were used as runabouts. The forklift and Vicente's 4 x 4 were quite new.

The mechanic seemed very competent, but must have been under pressure at times, to look after all those vehicles.

Over lunch with Maria at a nearby bar, each answered the other's questions and warmed to one another … Maria was a 33-year-old divorcee, with a ten-year-old son, Carlos, who loved football.

After lunch, Maria gave Robert a financial background to the business, with details of the transport operation.

As the days went by, Robert recorded copious notes, making telephone calls and visiting the garage.

Each day, Maria would sit down with him and together they not only developed a proposal but grew to know and respect each other more and more.

When Maria did things, they had a purpose. Robert learned to recognise the different sounds of her approaching footsteps ... the normal sound ... and the staccato clip clop announcing that she had a purpose. When she was on a special mission, he didn't necessarily know what it was, but wanted to know ... and would soon find out!

Maria would catch men looking too long at her small trim figure or too deeply into her dark eyes. She would return their gaze, then slowly but firmly enunciate their name in a sultry tone.

He noticed that, first, her breasts would lift as she breathed deeply, then, as she exhaled, she would say ...

"R o b e r t o !" and when she spoke like that to him, he would feel a warmth at the back of his neck and his heart would miss a beat.

At progress meetings with Vicente, Robert and Maria were able to establish what additional finance Vicente was prepared to invest. After only two weeks, Robert was determined to make the plan work and gave his employer final notice of his intention to leave. The next week, they set their joint proposal before Vicente.

The proposal surprised Vicente with its option for Robert to make a significant investment in the new company.

Finally, after lengthy discussions over several days, it was agreed to begin by buying one new long-distance truck which Robert would drive. If this was successful, Robert would make an investment to enable the purchase of a second truck, on the understanding that two new drivers and an additional garage mechanic would be employed, so that Robert could also manage the other aspects of the transport business.

In July, 1998, Robert and Vicente made joint visits to potential buyers of their fresh produce, proposing direct delivery at competitive prices which would include delivery.

They succeeded in winning new clients in England and early in September, 1998, Robert made his first delivery in the company's new truck.

Maria's son, Carlos, was a slim handsome intelligent boy, with a way of winning without conflict. He made friends easily and loved basketball and football. He was now almost as tall as Maria and played football, as goalkeeper, for the local youth team, although most of the other players were older. His football hero was Real Madrid's new nineteen-year-old goalkeeper, Iker Casillas.

Carlos thought the youth team was playing better since the new English trainer had joined them and he noticed that his mother was now coming more often to see their matches.

Spain was doing well in the football world cup and Maria invited Roberto to join her and Carlos to see the next match on television. After the match, they celebrated Spain's success over some tapas. Later, as they finished the bottle of wine, which Roberto had brought, they talked, partly in Spanish and partly in English, about life in Andalucía.

That was the evening when they started to become a family.

It became more than a blossoming romance between Roberto and Maria, because Carlos soon looked upon Roberto as father, friend and sometimes co-conspirator in little schemes to involve the three of them.

One Saturday, they went to see Maria's family.

Roberto drove them to Córdoba in his new Nissan 4 x 4 ... down a narrow street and through an archway with enormous doors and into a tiny square, surrounded by old houses bedecked with bougainvillea and geraniums.

After parking the car, Maria and Carlos led Robert into a separate courtyard, adorned with more flowers.

Maria's mother, Esperanza, was waiting for them and greeted them with arms outstretched. She called out, *"Louis ... they're here."*

Instantly, chaos erupted as the whole family burst out into the courtyard ...

It was kisses and hugs all round as Maria introduced her mother and father, her sister and husband, her brother and wife and what seemed like a small army of young teenagers.

With a fatherly arm around Roberto's shoulders, Maria's father led them into the dining room, where an enormous oak table was tightly surrounded by 14 solid looking chairs.

Against one wall was an enormous display cabinet. The floor was covered with antique terracotta tiles. The walls were tiled, to a height of about a metre, with typical Andalucian tiles and the rest of the walls were white roughcast. There were heavy drapes at the windows and a couple of rustic oil paintings on the walls.

As they ate, Roberto learned that Maria's mother and father owned the adjacent small hotel, and that her brother, Fernando, had recently retired early from the Guardia Civil and was now the chef; his wife, Nuria, was the administrator and receptionist and they had two daughters.

He also learned that Maria's sister, Carmen, was a nurse, her husband, Tomas, was a physiotherapist in Granada and they had three daughters.

It was too much, however, for Roberto to remember the names of all five girls, but he knew that Fernando's younger daughter, the one who looked like a younger version of Maria, was called Sofia.

Later, the youngsters all disappeared and the adults talked animatedly until about 9 o'clock in the evening, when they all gathered around the table again for more food and drink.

In the early hours of Sunday morning, after most of the family, including Carlos, had retreated to their allocated rooms in the house, Maria's mother took them into the hotel and tactfully led them to adjoining rooms and wished them goodnight.

In the morning, they slowly gathered for a light breakfast, after which, farewells were made to Carmen, Tomas, and their three girls as they left for Granada.

Maria and Roberto left Carlos with his cousins, so that the two lovebirds were free to wander around, hand in hand, through the ancient streets, past houses adorned with displays of brightly coloured flowers.

They returned for a quiet lunch with Maria's mother and father, while Fernando and Nuria took up their hotel duties and Carlos was entertained by his cousins.

After lunch, they all said their goodbyes and the trio set off for their separate homes in Huercal Overa.

Throughout the winter of 98/99, Robert continued making deliveries to England, with the occasional return loads. He wanted to do a summer season before buying a second truck and engaging more employees.

The following April, during the Semana Santa festival, when the Jacaranda trees were announcing spring, Maria appeared in her traditional Andalucian costume, complete with a flower in her hair, and Roberto couldn't take his eyes off her.

She danced the graceful Sevillana and his heart raced.

A few days later, Maria agreed to marry Roberto and Carlos asked if Roberto would, at last, be moving in with them.

The answer was, *"yes."*

Robert's parents, Rosa and Colin, (now 68 and 72 respectively), were delighted to hear the news and, although the wedding was to be in Córdoba, plans were made for Robert to collect them from Almeria airport and establish them in his flat in Huércal Overa.

However, Maria's mother and father, Esperanza and Louis, insisted that they also come to Córdoba a week before the wedding, so they could get to know one another beforehand.

So, according to plan, towards the end of May 1999, Rosa and Colin established themselves in Robert's flat and spent some time with Robert, Maria and Carlos … Then, at the beginning of June, the five of them went in Robert's 4 x 4 to Córdoba, where Esperanza, showed them to their specially prepared rooms in the hotel, but gave Carlos his own favourite room in the family house.

Although Rosa was only a child when she left Spain, her adopted Spanish father, Leo, had spoken to her in Spanish whenever he could … It enabled Rosa to chat in Spanish and so 'the oldies' happily swapped stories about their families as they worked together, making preparations for the wedding.

*

In June, 1999, there must have been almost 80 guests at the wedding and reception, although only Rosa and Colin represented Robert's family.

A month before his twelfth birthday, Carlos was Best Man, although he sometimes needed help from his deputy, (his uncle Fernando).

Carlos proudly announced his approval of the marriage and complimented the bridesmaid, Sofia.

Roberto gave a short speech in English and then a

slightly longer one in halting Spanish.

Finally, he was received with loud applause when he said, in Spanish, *"My mother was born in Cordoba and my father in England, so my blood is half Spanish and half English ... BUT my **passion** is one hundred percent Spanish!"*

After the wedding, Robert, Maria, Carlos, Rosa and Colin returned to Huércal Overa and a few days later, Rosa and Colin returned to England and Robert moved into Maria's house.

The transport business was progressing to Robert's satisfaction and a 22-year-old mechanic was recruited. The journeys to England were increasing and, occasionally, Robert's previous company was used to provide additional runs.

It therefore followed that the proposed new transport company was formed. A new truck was ordered and an additional long-distance driver was recruited to drive the existing truck which Robert had been driving. When the new truck arrived, Robert drove it until a second long-distance driver started.

Winter passed and the New Year, (and new millennium), saw the expansion of the packing and distribution warehouse, and Robert gaining more clients for the transport company. In addition, two trailers were purchased to improve the collection of produce from the local growers.

Roberto succeeded in making the transport business into a separate company, with him and Vicente as directors and equal shareholders. The business flourished, more vehicles were bought and staff numbers were increased. Maria worked as office manager for both companies.

*

In July, 2000, for the 13th birthday of Carlos, they went to the Mini Hollywood theme park, in the nearby Tabernas desert. It was a replica western town, called Fort Bravo, which had been used as a film set for spaghetti westerns like Clint Eastwood's *A Fistful of Dollars* and was now a popular tourist attraction, including a re-enactment of the gunfight at the OK corral. It was a long day, but it was a good day out.

Happy endings for Rosa's family

Their Spanish hearts imbued a passion for family life.

Not far from the business, Robert and Maria bought a new villa, together with a small bungalow on an adjacent plot. This enabled Rosa and Colin to enjoy regular holidays near the family and, in 2001, they sold The Vicarage in England and move permanently to the bungalow.

Sometimes, in the following summers, the family enjoyed a day in Mojacar, both in the village on the hill and on the beach.

One very special outing was to Lorca, for the magical Semana Santa celebrations. The family left home after breakfast, and less than half an hour later, the castle dominated the skyline. It was originally built as an Arab citadel in the 13th century. They took a picnic lunch and explored the historic fortress castle, with its commanding view over a vast area. It was late afternoon when they ventured into the town itself.

Lorca Castle

They wandered around the town, which was crowded with tourists.

As darkness fell, they took their pre-booked seats in one of the viewing stands on the main street, the surface of which was covered with sand. Soon, all the viewing stands were filled with eager visitors from many countries.

The procession included Christian pageants, with groups of up to one hundred ceremonially dressed pallbearers, carrying enormous tributes to Christ and the Virgin Mary.

There were ladies, dressed in stunning costumes, elegantly depicting the Arab history of Lorca.

There were also charioteers, representing the Roman influence in Lorca. They raced down the main street and, to the thrill of the spectators, made dramatic stops by the viewing galleries. There were also spectacular feats of horsemanship to delight the viewers.

That explained why the road had been covered with sand!

The family were so impressed with the pageant that, in later years, they went again several times.

*

When Carlos finished school, he gained a degree at Murcia University. He was then accepted at the prestigious military flying school in San Javier and became an air force pilot.

ABOUT THE AUTHOR

When the author retired, he and his wife lived in Spain and France for 17 years. He developed a deep empathy for the Spanish people and their passion for life. He told his Spanish friends, *"My passport is British, but my heart is Spanish."*

Printed in Great Britain
by Amazon

59905747R00132